CRAFTING AN ALIBI

Gasper's Cove Mysteries Book 5

BARBARA EMODI

C&T PUBLISHING
Another Maker Inspired!

Gasper's Cove Mysteries Series

DEDICATION

*To Ron Ryckman. Dog-walker, firefighter,
builder of many things, and gentleman.*

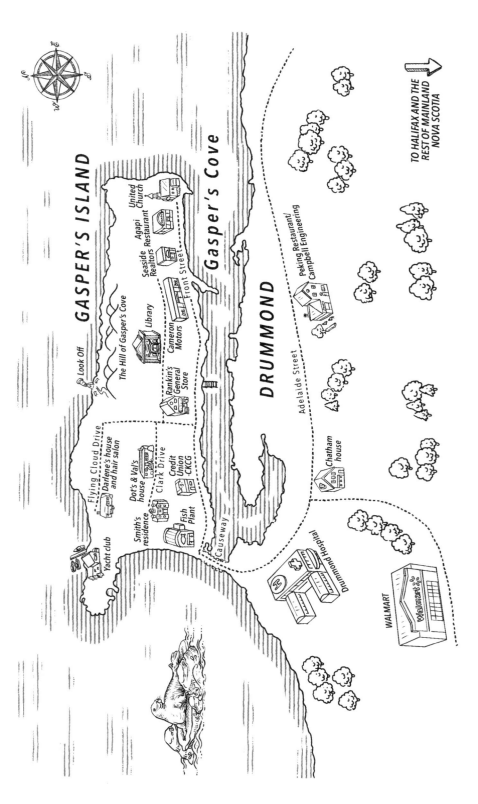

CHAPTER ONE

"We need cash," Joyce said, prim and upright in her seasonal cardigan, knitted maple leaves accented by a gold cat brooch she'd worn for sixty years. "And fast."

"We have a business proposition for you," Bernadette added. "We have no one else to ask. You're my great-niece. I told the girls you'll keep this a secret."

Next to her, Minnie, the third member of the group, nodded. "That's right. We know people say you're quick to fly off the handle, but we know you never let anyone down. And not many folks would understand our situation. We think you will."

I put my china teacup down. I laid the tiny silver spoon on the saucer. This was not what I had expected when the ladies of Seaview Manor invited me for tea.

"I am not sure I understand," I said. I'd known these three women my whole life. Each of them must be close to ninety. If I was going to get more information, I would have to be delicate about it. "Isn't everything here covered?" I asked. "By the province and your Canada pensions? Accommodations and meals?" What financial worries would these ladies have at this stage of their lives? The community had and would always take care of them. We'd built the Manor so our seniors could stay with us, here on Gasper's Island. No one wanted grandparents too frail to live with family to go across the causeway to Drummond or, even worse, somewhere else down the road in mainland Nova Scotia.

Minnie waved my question aside with her hand, her rings loose on her fingers. She'd dressed up for this meeting in a well-preserved red wool flannel jacket she'd made herself. Above her covered buttons, a rhinestone brooch and heavy clip-on earrings glinted in the sun that slid in sideways from windows that faced the bright waters of the North Atlantic.

"We're fine, thank you," Minnie said, snapping the crimson bows of her lips shut. I had insulted her. "The money's not for us, it's for the young people."

Bernadette leaned forward, the fringed tie of a crocheted vest skimming the surface of the tea in her cup. "Between us, we have twenty-three grandchildren and great-grandchildren."

Joyce picked up the teapot and poured. Minnie put another butter tart on my plate. It looked homemade, the top of a crispy raisin visible in a crack of a filling made of butter, brown sugar, and eggs.

I was being bribed. It was working. I took a bite and listened.

"And that's not counting the nieces and nephews, and some of them are grandparents themselves," Joyce continued. "It all adds up."

"You bet it does," Minnie nodded. "Birthdays, Christmases, graduations, bridal showers, christenings. These days, cards cost more than the five dollars you put in them."

"And the cats," Joyce reminded the table. "Let's not forget the SPCA." She pushed her chair back, and as if it had been waiting for an entry line, a rangy gray cat jumped up on her lap.

"Who's that?" I asked. "It looks like Shadow's cousin, exactly the same shade of gray." Shadow was our store cat who lived down at the family store I managed, Rankin's General. Originally brought in to chase away visiting mice, Shadow spent most of her time dozing on the quilts we sold upstairs in the Crafters' Co-op.

"He could be related," Joyce agreed. "Gasper's Cove cats tend to be gray. Passed on, one generation to another, all got the same look about them."

"Like us," Bernadette observed. "Valerie here's got the Rankin eyes, one blue and one green. Dark curly hair. A touch of the fey, the curse to feel premonitions. Our childbearing hips. There's a word for it. What is it?"

"Genetics," I said, reaching out to stroke the fine, soft gray fur. I wouldn't have described my figure quite like that. "I didn't know you had a cat in here."

"Maybelline sent him," Joyce said, referring to a long-gone black cat I had seen in Joyce's tearoom and alteration shop when I was a child. In those days, Joyce used to read the leaves in her customers' cups. She claimed that Maybelline had been her spiritual guide and that, one way or another, the cat had never left her.

"Maybe you're right," I said. It was the best I could do. "What's this one called?"

"Max Factor," Joyce said, as if stating the obvious. "He's a boy."

"Keeps us all company," Bernadette said. "Now, back to the money. Family costs," she looked sideways at Minnie, "and some of us have inventor grandsons."

"A good investment." Minnie was proud. "Big Bob is a thinker. Why did you think Alexander Graham Bell spent his summers here and moved to Cape Breton when he retired? Nova Scotians are deep thinkers. We have given the world its best ideas."

"And those are?" Joyce asked, giving me a wink. I had a feeling this was not the first time they had had this conversation.

I was right. Minnie was quick to answer. "One, we invented the portable ironing board. Two, a man in Halifax came up with the idea for backup lights for cars. Three, well, three was the big one."

"Which was? Don't tell me it was something Bob came up with," Joyce said, teasing Minnie for my benefit.

"No, it wasn't his idea," Minnie admitted. "It could have been, but someone else got there first." She paused. "Number three is hockey. Invented in Windsor, Nova Scotia, 1800."

"You got a point there. That's one idea that caught on," Joyce conceded. She scanned the empty dining room for eavesdroppers. "This is all very educational for Valerie, but we should get back to business. Our proposal."

"I'm listening," I said, distracted and impressed by the butter tart. It wasn't easy to make a pastry strong enough to contain a heavy filling and keep it this flakey. "Who made these?" I asked.

"My niece," Joyce answered, then lowered her voice to a whisper. "I'll get her to make you some. But listen. We have inventory we want to unload."

"Something we've been hiding for years," Bernadette added.

"Keeping it for emergencies," Minnie said.

"We didn't want to touch the capital." Joyce reasserted herself as chief negotiator. "But at our age, with our expenses ..."

"It's time," Bernadette interrupted. She had the most grandchildren. "You are the only person we trust to sell it."

"Sell what?" I asked. Did they mean at the store in the Crafters' Co-op? What were we discussing? Knitted socks? Tatted doilies?

"We'll get to the what in a minute." Bernadette looked to her partners for reassurance before she continued. "But whatever we tell you today has to stay between us."

I looked outside at the view. It was a beautiful crisp day, one of the last of the summer. Perfect for a dog walk. Toby and I could drive to the north shore of the island and walk the beach. Agreeing to sell mitts shouldn't take long.

"Between us," I promised.

"Good," Joyce said. "Because there's one little problem with our goods."

"What's that?" I asked.

Joyce hesitated.

Minnie stepped in. She'd never had a business like Joyce, but she'd run a household for more than half a century on a fisherman's wages. She wasn't shy about talking dollars.

"What we're looking to get onto the market is valuable. But the thing is," she sighed, "we stole it."

CHAPTER TWO

I hid my open mouth with an embroidered napkin. "Excuse me?"

"It was years ago," Bernadette explained. "Not here. We went to the city, into Halifax," she added, as if this made the crime acceptable. "We were on a bit of a tear. It was like something you and Darlene would do," she said, referring to me and her granddaughter, my best friend.

This was not reassuring. Darlene and I had been up to a few things in our time, some of which we regretted, most of which we did not tell our mothers or grandmothers.

"Our current problem is we want to liquidate these assets," Minnie continued. Like me, she had a son who was an accountant and had picked up how to talk like one. "But at our age, we don't want to be charged."

"Charged?" I asked. It was hard to keep up with these ladies. "What for?"

"Burglary, my dear," Joyce said. "Break and enter. We took something that didn't belong to us and brought it home. Put it away. But now it's time."

"Time?" I echoed. "For what?"

Bernadette patted my hand. "To let it go," she said. "But in a way that it can't be traced back to our group. That's why we want you to help us."

I eyed the remaining butter tarts on the blue and white china plate. An old design, probably Spode, undoubtedly valuable. "Maybe you should tell me the whole story," I said, reaching for one of the larger tarts. "Right from the beginning. Don't leave anything out."

Joyce lifted the lid of the teapot and pretended to examine what was left inside. "Did your mother ever take you into Halifax to Drysdale's?" she asked. "On Spring Garden Road?"

"She sure did. A couple of times a year, whenever she was sewing something special," I answered. Who could forget a trip to Drysdale's Fine Fabrics? "The first time, I was ten. We went for fabric to make dresses for Darlene and me for Jenny's wedding." Jenny was a relative from a branch of the family who had gone to work in the textile mills of Lowell, Massachusetts, in the 1930s but, as many did, came home every summer. And like many of the American cousins, Jenny had wanted to be married in Gasper's Cove.

Bernadette laughed. "I remember that wedding. You and Darlene were terrible flower girls. You giggled so much you could hardly stand up. No one could hear the vows. And then you knocked over the flower stands." She stopped to wipe the tears from her eyes. "I got to say, though, you both looked nice. Real silk satin, those outfits."

I smiled at the memory. My mother had sewn my dress. Bernadette's oldest daughter, Darlene's mother, Colleen, had made hers.

"My mom had such a thing about good fabric," I said. "That's why we went to Drysdale's." Even after all this time, the memory of those gorgeous bolts of fabric, Viyella shirting, Belgian lace, and Egyptian cotton, all on long tables or stacked on mahogany shelves along the walls, made me feel faint. "You're going to think I am crazy, but sometimes I wish I could travel back in time just to buy fabric. There's nothing like that around anymore."

The ladies exchanged a look.

"We are so glad you feel that way," Joyce said, carefully, "because you might see that fabric again."

"What do you mean?" I asked.

"The Drysdales were related to us, on my dad's side," Minnie began. "You probably know that."

"Yes, I do," I said. A trace of old gossip nudged at me, some kind of a falling-out. "And wasn't their store in Halifax in the family, like ours was here?" Rankin's had been a fixture in Gasper's Cove for more than a century, just like Drysdale's had been in the city.

"You got that right," Bernadette said. "But the Drysdales weren't like the Rankins. They were the ones with the big ideas. Looked down on us and said all we did was the same old, same old. Anyway, after the war, when the Drysdale boys came back, they lived it up. Fancy houses."

"And even fancier women," Minnie sniffed. "Boats so big they couldn't sail them by themselves. Bills they couldn't pay. And as things went along, Drysdale after Drysdale didn't get any smarter. Eventually, there was nothing left. The family had to sell."

It came back to me then. It must have been around Thanksgiving, the fall after the wedding. I was in bed at home, but the adults were still up, talking in the living room. Their words had flowed down the hall, the voices raised, and not just from the rum. "Over my dead body," I'd heard an uncle say. "Never going to let that happen to us." Someone else, an older voice, had added, "What's in the family stays in the family." Another voice had made a toast. I heard the glasses clink. I went to sleep that night secure that my world would never change. And later, when it was my turn to manage the store, and changing times had put our future at risk, I had made sure it hadn't. The Crafters' Co-op had kept Rankin's General afloat. I'd kept the promise.

It seemed the Drysdales hadn't. I returned to the present.

"So, what happened next?" I asked.

"When the news got to Gasper's Cove that the Drysdales had sold Fine Fabrics to a bankruptcy broker, we knew we had to do something," Joyce said. "We," she swept an arm around the table, "decided we couldn't let all that beautiful fabric be shipped off and marked down by people who didn't know what it was."

Minnie took over. It was time for the details. "I worked there one summer as a girl," she said. "They sent me to stay with a cousin in Halifax for the two months. When I left, no one asked me for my key."

They let this sink in.

"We figured those dummies hadn't changed the locks in all those years," Bernadette explained. "Never did know how to run a business."

I took the last tart. "What did you do?" I asked, holding my hand up to catch the crumbs.

Minnie took a big breath, "You have to understand," she said, "the stage we were at then. The change of life. It can make you angry."

"And brave," Joyce added. "Irritable and courageous. It will be your turn one day. You'll see."

I kept listening.

"We borrowed one of the men's trucks, and the three of us went down to Halifax. It was a Sunday; the stores were closed. We pulled up out back ...," Bernadette said.

"The key still worked—no surprise there," Minnie continued. "We went right in, and we liberated that fabric. Brought it home and put it into hiding."

I stared at the three women and saw they were telling me the truth. "But your families, your husbands, didn't anyone ask why you'd gone to the city?" I asked. "Or noticed you'd come back with a truckload of fabric?"

Bernadette laughed. "No. We told the men we were going to see a friend who was having a lady's operation. We knew that would shut down any questions."

"And before we got back into town, we stopped on the way. We wrapped the bolts up in tarps and put them in a hiding place we knew about in one of the old rumrunners' cottages. No one locked doors," Joyce said. "We did a good job; we wanted it to stay dry."

"Didn't you worry you'd get caught?" I asked.

Bernadette seemed surprised by the question. "What do you mean? We had the perfect alibi."

"You did? What was it?"

"That we were housewives," Minnie explained. "In those days, that meant no one thought we were capable of doing much more than dusting. Not that some of us spent a lot of time on that." She tried to wink, but her mascaraed lids temporarily stuck together.

Joyce leaned forward. "There's power in being underestimated," she said. "You can get away with a lot because no one really sees you or notices what you are doing."

"And that gets even better the older you get," Bernadette added, "but we don't move around like we used to. That's why we need you to go out and get this fabric we put away and sell it. And then give us the money, if you don't mind. We will give you exact instructions on where to look."

"I can't do it," I said. "I'm sorry." I couldn't get involved in this crazy scheme, even though a part of me wanted to see what they'd taken.

Joyce ignored my protests. "No rush," she said. "Any time you can go out this week will be fine."

"It's been there long enough," Bernadette agreed. "What's another few days? The place has been through a few hands since we were there, but if anyone found our stash, we would have heard."

"Take anything you like and keep it," Joyce said. "For your troubles."

Minnie saw me waver and moved in. She was evidently the group's closer. "Did we tell you about the camel's hair coating, brushed?" she asked. "Silk organza, pre-pleated? Wool from Scotland?"

"Wool?" That got my attention. "What kind of wool?"

Minnie looked at her partners and turned over her best card. "Harris tweed. From the Outer Hebrides. Spun and woven in crofters' cottages."

I looked at Bernadette, Minnie, and Joyce. They had me. We all knew that. "I can't go into some stranger's cottage and start digging around for stolen goods," I said.

Joyce reached over and patted my arm. "You have every right to be there. You know the owners."

"I do?" I asked. "Who?"

"Your children," Bernadette said. "Our treasure is in your family cottage. You just didn't know it."

CHAPTER THREE

After my disturbing tea party at Seaview Manor, I went home, picked up my golden retriever, Toby, and drove down the hill to our store on Front Street, situated opposite the wharf and facing the town of Drummond across the water and the causeway. Toby and I were a unit. We lived together, and we worked together, myself as manager of Rankin's General and the Co-op, Toby as the store greeter from his post on an old recliner inside the front entrance.

My aunt Colleen, Bernadette's daughter and Darlene's mother, was busy at the cash counter when we arrived. She had a map of the area spread out in front of her and was explaining to two visitors in wide-brimmed hats complete with drawstrings exactly where they were. At the rear of the store, near the stairs out to the small parking lot, I heard heavy thumping. I sighed because I knew what this meant. Fall was on its way. Winter was not far behind. Our handyman, Duck Macdonald, would be on the back landing, moving out the heavy bags of peat moss and soil and moving in sacks of salt and sand, ready for the ice.

Summer in Nova Scotia was spectacular, magical, and perfect, but it was too short. That, the locals claimed, was the whole point. The dreary things in life make a person appreciate the good, they argued. I looked up at the pressed metal ceilings of the old store and down at the weathered boards on the floor, worn so they dipped in the middle, rolling underfoot like waves, and I knew the old-timers were right. The store, like all of us, had seen many years, many seasons, and many families made, grown, and gone. My own three children had moved away. Kay was in Aberdeen, Scotland. Paul, once a law student, was now a vegan baker in Brooklyn. My middle boy, Chester, worked in investments in Toronto. But this summer, they had all been back, staying at a place that they bought together. That cottage had changed everything. So, as discouraging as it was to hear Duck throwing around the bags of salt, I was able to remind myself that my winters would now lead to times when my family would be back. I wanted to protect the simplicity of those future summers. I'd look in the cottage for whatever the Seaview ladies had stashed there years ago, deal with the past for them, and then move on.

I wasn't able to think about family for long. The bell over the big front door chimed. And Wade Corkum of the Royal Canadian Mounted Police walked into the store.

I went to meet him. I'd known Wade since high school, back when he'd had hair. I'd seen Wade ride high when he was an almost hockey star and watched him sink low when a bad shoulder took that away. I'd been there, too, when Wade pulled himself together and joined the RCMP, to play a different kind of defense. What they used to say about Wade at the rink was still true: He had heart. Not a bad quality to have in anyone enforcing the law.

"You're back," I greeted him. "How was Toronto? And the Maple Leafs?" Wade had been away from Gasper's Cove for a season. An old teammate, now the hockey team's assistant coach, had needed help with rookie training. Wade had some time off, extended after he'd been hurt on the job, and accepted the offer.

"The new guys were great. The big city, not so much. I'm glad to be back." Wade paused as if he had something to say but didn't know how to say it. "Least I got a chance to catch up with CJ."

CJ? This was the name my son Chester had invented for himself in Toronto, a combination of the initials of his first name and his middle one, James.

"You did?" I asked. This was news to me. I didn't know my son and Wade had stayed in touch.

"Question for you," Wade said, instead of answering me. "You always seem to know what's going on."

"True enough," I said. I took this as a compliment and, since it came from the RCMP, also an endorsement of my observational skills, which in the past had not always been appreciated. "What's happening?"

"It may be a seasonal thing, but we're seeing an uptick in home robberies and random arson, a few sheds, an old car parked behind a building, things like that." Wade shook his head. Recreational vandalism or trouble-making was beyond his understanding. "It all seems to be in or around remote houses or vacation places and rentals when they're unoccupied. The weird part about the robberies is that what has been taken makes no sense. I mean, one guy reported someone had removed his mallard ducks from the wall. You know, the china birds that look like they're flying?"

I did. We'd had a set at home when I was growing up. "Seems a weird thing to steal," I said.

"I know," Wade agreed. "That's why I think it's bored teenagers. Who else would leave a Rolex watch but take an old quilt off only one of the beds? We're not talking criminal masterminds here."

"I see your point," I said. "But how do I figure in all of this?" I hoped Wade would repeat the part about how I had investigative talents, but he didn't.

The RCMP officer sighed. "It was CJ's suggestion I talk to you," he admitted. "We're not agreeing on this, but he's got some idea there's a pattern to what's going on. He thought you might have noticed something."

I was surprised. Chester played hockey with Wade in Toronto, but how did that make him an RCMP advisor?

"Noticed what?" I asked. I was flattered that my son thought I could be useful. That didn't happen much anymore.

"Not sure. I'm covering all bases. It's a long shot, but in case it's not kids ... after all, you do get all the locals and tourists in here." Wade picked up a Nova Scotia bumper sticker from the stack on the counter. "I got to ask. Anyone around seem kind of odd?"

I thought about this. *Odd* didn't narrow things down much in rural Nova Scotia. Wade must mean criminally odd, not just eccentric.

"Like someone buying hammers and crowbars so they could break in?" I asked, warming to the subject. "Or bricks to smash in windows? Burlap bags to carry away loot?" It was too early for ski masks, but we did carry camouflage jackets. I could see why the RCMP had come to me.

"Nothing like that." Wade swept my questions away with a large, scarred hand. "No bricks. No hammers. So far, there haven't been any signs of forced entry. That's what's strange. I'm only asking because ... look, Val, I'll come out and say it. You get into people's business. Sometimes you hit the panic button. But if anyone's around who might be up to no good, I know you'd pick up on it. And if that happens, don't do anything. Just call me."

I wasn't sure if I should feel insulted by Wade's suggestion that I was a busybody. I decided it didn't matter. I liked to be involved.

"Speed dial," I said. "Anyone shifty shows up, you'll be the first to know."

And then on cue, the shiftiest resident of Gasper's Cove, Nova Scotia, walked in.

CHAPTER FOUR

"Hey, Wade," Harry Sutherland grinned. "You turn the Leafs around? Gonna win the Stanley Cup this year?"

Wade winced. The Toronto Maple Leafs hadn't won the Stanley Cup since 1967, the longest drought in the National Hockey League's history. Being more north–south than east–west in their orientation, most of the locals were Boston Bruins fans. The persistent failure of a hockey team from an area of Canada that referred to Nova Scotia as a have-not province gave them much satisfaction.

"You never know," Wade conceded. "Some of the new guys they've signed up are pretty good."

He squared his shoulders, pushing out a black padded vest with *Police* on the front of it, and tried to stare Harry down. That had no effect. Over the course of his life, those in positions of responsibility—family, teachers, employers, and government representatives—had tried to assert some sort of authority over Harry. None had succeeded. To reinforce that point, Harry ambled away from Wade, whistling, secure that on the subject of the Toronto Maple Leafs, at least, he'd had the last word.

Wade watched him go. When Harry was out of sight down the sundries aisle, he looked at me. "I'm off now, Valerie. Remember, anything unusual, let us know."

"You bet on it," I said.

Wade nodded, slapped his hat on the shiny dome of his shaved head, and strode out of the store to the patrol car at the curb.

As soon as he was gone, Harry drifted back. "That guy there could have been one of the great ones," he pronounced with the certainty of someone who would know. Harry worked at the local yacht club in the summer but in the winter drove the Zamboni at the arena, resurfacing the ice between games. Because of his work with the ice resurfacer, he considered himself one of Canada's hockey insiders. "That guy's spent his whole life thinking he missed out on the National Hockey League," Harry said, nudging me in the side as if sharing a secret. "But maybe the NHL missed out on Wade. I wonder if he ever thought of that?" Harry crossed his arms. "Better to blossom where you're planted. Like I did."

I didn't know what to say to such a profound observation, so I retreated to store manager chitchat.

"What can I do for you today, Harry?" I asked. "Something you need for the yacht club? How are things going over there with the new manager, anyway?"

Harry surveyed the empty store to see if anyone could hear him.

"Terrible, if you want to know the truth, just terrible," he whispered. "That new general manager? The one they brought in that I am supposed to report to? The big shot who thinks he knows what he's doing? Ha. The guy knows zip. He'll never last. There's blood in the water over there, I can tell you. Members want it back the way it used to be, when it was just me running things."

I didn't think that would happen. The truth was, Gasper's Cove was changing, and parts of it would never be the same, whether Harry liked it or not. Many of our visitors had come here for a season and then became permanent residents. As a result, the yacht club had grown to a scale where it needed full-time professional management and not a summer refugee from the hockey rink. Every year, the simple old lobster boats, outfitted for sunset family cruises, and the 30-footers owned by local sailors like Stuart Campbell, an engineer I sometimes thought about, were becoming outnumbered by bigger boats, many with out-of-province flags at the stern, to show where they'd come from and to where they'd return. None of us had been surprised when we'd heard that the new manager, Peter Tupper, an early retiree from the civil service, had demoted Harry from a position of influence to instead wiping down the counter at the bar, a job he supplemented by doing odd jobs around the community.

"Maybe you should give the new guy a chance," I suggested. "Sometimes you have to accept some change so the big things can stay the same. Look at this store," I waved my arms wide. "We still sell hardware and tools, but it wasn't enough to keep us going. That's why we opened the Crafters' Co-op upstairs. It pays the bills."

Harry sniffed. "You're not getting it. Peter Tupper, Mr. Nova Scotia Know-It-All, doesn't understand that just because he was a member of a golf course down in Halifax doesn't mean he knows what sailors want in a club, I can tell you that." Harry, a man himself unable to stand on a dock without getting seasick, drew himself up to his full five feet six inches. "There's going to be a mutiny, I tell ya. Members are talking."

"Like who?" I asked.

"The mayor, for one, Elliot Carter," Harry said. "Peter took away his commodore parking space and made me remove the special buoy we had painted up for his boat. He told Elliot the GM's role made a commodore redundant. Elliot's fit to be tied. I got a feeling that *redundant* is not a word he likes. I guess they made him redundant all the time when he worked for the province before he came here." Harry leaned in closer. "I think Elliot's got a touch of the nerves; the man hates it when anyone pulls rank. I figured it out. He gets triggered from feeling no one appreciates him. My friend down at the counter at the Motor Vehicle Registry says it's rampant in the government. That's another reason why I stayed out of the bureaucracy."

I ignored Harry's newest description of his nonexistent career plan. "That's Elliot," I said. "He tends to get huffy. But who else is upset? I mean, rules are rules."

"Not if they hurt people," Harry said. "Take old guys like Tommy Hirtle. Only trying to get by, that one. His wife's seventy-five, and she's still cleaning houses. Tommy's doing what he can, selling wood off their lot and helping folks get raccoons out of attics." He paused, letting me as a woman catch up with the significance of this. "That's skilled and dangerous work, you know. A raccoon never stops thinking. They like to stay one step ahead."

Yes, I knew about raccoons. We'd had them once in the attic. "That's true about raccoons. What does any of that have to do with the yacht club?" I asked.

"Everything. Money," Harry explained. "We never charged Tommy to moor his boat, but Peter told him to pay up or he'd have to leave." Harry shook his head in disgust. "You didn't hear it from me, but your buddy Stuart got Tommy hired to deal with the raccoons down there. Pay it off."

That sounded like something Stuart would do. "Things will settle down," I said, trying to appease Harry, which I knew would go nowhere. "I'm sure Peter will be good with the visitors. He'll talk their language."

Harry snorted. "Sure, if their language is yelling. You should have heard him go after that lady who does the séances—they knew each other from before, I think. Anyway, she said he didn't own the past. And she'd know. I mean, because of her business."

"Her business?" I asked, "Who are you talking about?"

"The one rented your kid's place," Harry looked surprised, as if I should know her. "She's a medium. Nice lady, she gave me good advice."

"She did?" I tried to remember if I had seen any new spiritualists in town. She must be one of the short-term rentals Chester organized when none of the family was here.

"Yup. Me and my mom went to her. I think Mom wanted to see if she could talk to Dad. Her best tablecloth's gone missing, and she's losing her mind over it. It was a wedding present. She thought Dad might know where it was. I went along because you know me, always an open mind. And besides, it was discount Tuesday for psychic services."

"Did your mom get through to your dad?" I asked. Harry's dad had been gone now for more than a decade at least. That was a long time to look for a tablecloth.

"Not sure about that," Harry said. "Dad was a man of few words at the best of times. But Twyla looked at some cards for me. Pretty interesting. She said they showed I was resourceful, which I am, with all the multitasking I take on. And optimistic, I checked that box too. The last card made her nervous, but I didn't mind it." Harry shrugged. "Always was into the martial arts myself."

"What do you mean?" I asked.

"Five swords," Harry answered. "Trouble, conflict. Everything I told you about the yacht club," he paused, "and one other thing. What was it? Oh, yeah. Revenge."

CHAPTER FIVE

No other customer we had the rest of that day was as interesting as Harry.

Duck and I sold 15 meters of lobster rope. Colleen tried to help a homeowner find doorknobs. Two visitors went up to the Co-op and came down with a pair of thrummed mittens. When they didn't understand why there was wool roving tufted inside, Colleen pulled out a pair she was working on and demonstrated the technique. That sold another half dozen pairs, destined for Boston and Christmas. When they left, I flipped over our *Open* side in the front window to *Closed*, collected Toby, and went to lock up. Colleen came up and stood beside me.

"I need to talk to you about Darlene," she said. "I'm worried."

I told Toby to sit.

My cousin and best friend and I talked every day. Nothing was going on that I could think of that would concern her mother. After all, Darlene was finally going to marry George Kosoulos, the future owner of the Agapi restaurant, if his mother and father ever retired, the man she should have married decades ago.

"What about?" I asked. "Darlene's in great shape."

"Is she?" Colleen asked. "Then why won't she set a date for the wedding?" She took off her turquoise glasses and held them out at arm's length, looking for smudges, stalling for time. "This will be Darlene's fourth trip to the altar. You'd think she'd have it down pat by now. But she tunes out when I want to talk arrangements. Something's up. She won't tell me what it is."

"I can talk to her," I said. Colleen was a mother. All mothers worried. About things that didn't exist or matters that were none of their business. I should know. This was one of my own areas of expertise. "But what if what's bothering Darlene is something she's not ready to tell you?" I asked. "Then what do you want me to do?"

Colleen looked amazed at the question. "What you always do when there's a problem. You fix it."

The next morning, I sat in my kitchen, looked out at my maple trees, already showing a few red leaves, and drank my coffee. I thought about my conversation with Colleen. I wondered what it was about me that got me so involved in other people's lives. Colleen wanted to know what was going on with her daughter, and she'd asked me to find that out. The ladies at Seaview Manor had extended families they loved and trusted, and yet they had shared their secret with only me and asked for my help. And even Wade, who in the past had found my attempts to help the RCMP annoying, wanted me to keep an eye out for random vandals.

Why me?

Was it because I was single and at an age when people thought I had more time than I did? Was it because of the store? Did being the manager put me in the middle of all Gasper's Cove activity? Or was it my naturally nosey personality? Curious people were always good listeners. Or was it more basic? Did I just need to be needed, and it showed?

I had no idea.

I stood up and put my cup in the sink. I didn't have time to think about myself. I'd promised Joyce, Bernadette, and Minnie I'd go look for their stolen fabric. I settled Toby down with a new yak bone and headed to the door. I didn't want this job. The sooner it was over, the better.

In the car, I buckled my seatbelt, and I read Joyce's note one more time. It was written in a beautiful, graceful cursive, a pleasure to read. No one was taught how to write that way anymore.

Go to the pantry in the kitchen. Pull out the bottom two shelves on the back wall. Be careful. On the wall behind the shelves is a little latch. Push hard. It should open. You will see a cupboard. Inside are old papers, a few bottles of rum (we took some home), and the rolled tarps. The bolts of fabric are inside. We did them up tight because we put down mothballs to keep out the mice. I hope that worked. Don't mind the smell.

I put my key in the ignition and tried to see the cottage's kitchen in my mind. The old house had been built in the traditional way, with rooms added when they were needed, put wherever they fit. This method in country homes produced rabbit-warren interiors. Hallways on angles, bedrooms tacked onto kitchens, outside sheds connected and repurposed into storage rooms, laundries, bathrooms, or, as in this case, pantries. It wouldn't be hard to build a hiding place into such architectural confusion, or to live with a secret space there and not know it existed.

My phone was on the passenger seat next to my bag. I picked it up and checked it. Chester managed the rental of the cottage when the kids didn't need it. Peter Tupper from the yacht club, in fact, had wanted to take it for the year, but they'd opted for short-term rentals instead. Chester shared the booking calendar with me. That way, I knew when not to go into the cottage. I scrolled to this month and noted one new change. A Twyla Waters, who I figured must be Harry's medium, and who had stayed at the cottage in the spring, was taking it again for the upcoming weekend but had changed her booking to an early arrival just last night.

That meant she was there now.

I hadn't anticipated this. What excuse could I use for turning up and rummaging around a renter's pantry? I backed out of the driveway and tried to think of a story as I drove up the hill to the north side of the island. I looked to the ocean and the seagulls for inspiration, but they ignored me. I lowered my window to the onshore breeze and hoped it would whisper me an answer.

But all I could smell was smoke. And all I heard was a siren.

The wail came from behind me. It made me worry there had been a fire down at the wharf. But as I drove farther away from town, the louder the siren sounded.

It was following me.

That wasn't right.

Close to the road to the cottage, I looked in the rearview mirror. A few turns back, I caught sight of a fire truck. Where was it going? As I drove down the dirt road to our property, I checked again, expecting to see the truck as it went by. Instead, I saw it veer off onto the same road I was on. I pulled over into a turnaround on the shoulder and let it shriek past. I felt terrible anxiety then, and fear. I turned back onto the road and moved ahead as quickly as I could, in a panic, so close behind the truck that the branches it snapped off as it traveled bounced off my windshield.

I knew this road.

I knew this route.

I knew this address.

I knew the trees would soon part at a clearing. At a perfect place to build, or buy, a summer place. Up high on a lot above the ocean, where it would make the most of the view.

We arrived at my family cottage, the fire truck and I, moments apart.

The truck pulled to the right side of the lawn, close to the Adirondack chairs I had sat in a few weeks before, and slammed to a stop. I parked a short distance away, half on the grass and half on the lane that led to the front door, next to the garbage bin and blue bags of recycling.

That door was gone now, as was most of the rest of the building.

The firetruck was too late, and so was I.

What had once been a family cabin was not there. Only angry rubble, as if it had been dropped from the sky, remained. The little place where we had shared time as a family was now only an outline on the cracked concrete footing, posts in each corner covered in a black, terrible bark. The breeze was strong, but the smell of the fire remained in the air. I noticed two vehicles, one a small car and the other a van with *Flynn's Surveying* on the side, both with the red and white license plates of the Nova Scotia volunteer fire department, parked back near the bushes.

Suddenly, the siren stopped, and the silence seemed even louder. The men were down. One of the locals, in a khaki jacket marked with the reflective tape of a volunteer, moved to lead them gingerly through the debris to what had once been the back of the building. One of the firemen from the truck stopped to open the hatch to the on-board reservoir of water but walked away. The long auxiliary hose used to draft water from a lake or the ocean remained coiled in the back of the truck. There was no fire left to put out.

I started to follow them. My legs were stiff at the knees. My body shook like I was outside in the winter without my coat. Tears were behind my eyes but wouldn't come out. I wanted to call out questions, but my breath was gone. I stumbled but kept going. I wanted to see. I wanted to understand.

A gnarled hand gripped my shoulder and stopped me.

"Can't be here, Valerie." The stiff fabric of Tommy Hirtle's protective gear was creased with use at the elbow. The old fisherman, I knew, had been with the volunteer fire department for years. "Property belongs to the department now," Tommy continued. "That's the law. As soon as the department arrives, it's ours. We've got to keep things secure." He looked at me, and his eyes flashed with understanding. "This is your family place now, isn't it? Your kids just bought it this year. I'm sorry." He hesitated, looked away, and forced himself to look back at me. "I hate to ask, but someone has to. Was anyone in the family staying here?"

I didn't understand the question. "They are all out of province. Why?" It was hard to breathe. I felt my throat closing in. It hit me then. "Oh no. There was a renter. Don't tell me someone was hurt." Now I was closer, I could see the corpse of my old couch, black springs all that was left of my housewarming contribution.

"Hurt? Afraid so. Renter, you say? I'll tell them that." Tommy looked up to study the clouds as if talking to them.

"What happened?" I reached out and grabbed Tommy's arm. I wasn't sure if it was to get his attention or for support. The horizon shimmered at the edge of my vision. What if one of my children had been here?

Tommy answered me slowly, starting at the beginning, avoiding the most important of my questions. "Alex, there," he pointed to the volunteer in the khaki jacket, "was out on the water early and saw the smoke. He called it in. Me and him live close, so we got here first. But we were too late. Must have started in the night." He paused to watch Alex with the other firefighters. "Tough on him. His first time. We found someone in bed in back. Smoke inhalation, I figure."

Twyla Waters. Our renter. A victim. A woman who had paid Chester to be here, on this night. Was there anything I could have done?

"But what started it?" I asked, hoping that more information would steady me. "It's too early for wood stoves."

"Hard to say. Most of the time, we never know." Tommy nodded at a row of blue bags set down next to one of the lidded garbage boxes used to keep bears and raccoons out of the trash. "But I have my thoughts." Even from a distance, I could see the wine bottles in the bag. "And this," he added, holding up a charred scrap of fabric I immediately recognized as genuine Harris tweed, "would have made a difference."

"Wool?" I blurted out. "What do you mean?"

"Wool, you say?" Tommy asked. "That might make it slow to catch, but it would make lots of smoke before there'd be any flame. Smoke would have killed 'em before they woke up." Tommy shook his head. "The old folks used to put anything they could find in these places for insulation. Newspaper, seaweed. Guess this time, it was cloth. One time we found a guy, maybe another one who had had a few, had been smoking in bed, fire went crazy. Know what he had in his wall?" He stopped and studied my face. I realized he was trying to distract me from looking at the wreckage.

"No idea," I said.

"Girlie magazines. Floor to ceiling." There was a hint of admiration in Tommy Hirtle's voice. "Some strange way to go."

I had to agree. I also had to leave. It hurt to be here. It was painful to see the destruction. One of the senior firefighters from Drummond noticed me and started to come my way. I knew he was going to ask me to leave, but I was ready to go anyway. I needed to call the kids. I had to talk to the ladies at Seaview Manor. I wanted to drive out of sight and cry. That cottage had brought my children home again, if only for the season. Now that the cottage was gone, I felt I was losing them all over again.

How could that happen?

My hurt was too deep for anyone to see it. I turned and walked away, with a backhand wave to Tommy as I went. I made my way through the long, uncut grass to my car, got in, locked the doors, and tried to feel safe. I was sitting there, trying to gather myself enough to drive home, when the surveyor's van lurched past, on its way out to the lane and the main road. As it went by, I saw the driver's face in profile, sandy beard, curly hair, and the khaki jacket. It was Alex, the volunteer who had found the body, probably Twyla's. Eyes in front of him, he looked shaken and grim. He was not, I realized, much younger than I was, but I didn't recognize him. Probably like so many, he had come to Gasper's Cove from away. I was sure when he came here, he hadn't been expecting this.

And neither had I. As I backed onto the lane, I took one last look at the place my offspring had bought for themselves in my world.

It was gone.

CHAPTER SIX

As soon as I got home, I called Chester. The other two had appointed him property manager. He was the only one who still lived in the country, and the best of the three of them with money. I would tell him about the fire first. He'd know what to do. It made me sad when I remembered he had been coming down for Thanksgiving in October to close the place up for the winter. Now that job would no longer need to be done, but many others would.

My call went to voicemail. I left a message.

It's your mom. Call me. Right away.

I waited up for Chester to phone back. When he didn't, I had a shower to wash the lingering smell of smoke from my hair and went to bed.

The next morning, I still hadn't heard from Chester. That left me feeling disappointed, annoyed, and restless. This was an emergency. Hadn't I made that clear? True, he often didn't call me back right away, but now it mattered. There was a time difference. He could be very busy at work. I struggled, then in the end, I decided to wait until noon and then try again.

I needed something to do in the meantime. Colleen and Duck had the morning shift at the store covered. But I wanted to move, to process what had happened. Finally, I got in the car and headed out to Seaview Manor. The least I could do was let the ladies know that their stolen nest egg was gone.

My meeting with Bernadette, Minnie, and Joyce did not go as well as I had planned. There were too many interruptions, and no one believed anything I said.

"You didn't have any trouble, did you?" Joyce asked as soon as I arrived in the Manor's dining room, apparently the ladies' headquarters. "With the secret door to the cubbyhole? The rumrunner who put it in was a shipwright, and he did a good job. But maybe after all this time ..."

I looked down at the tablecloth.

Bernadette caught my hesitation. "Did it stick? The salt air can be hard on hinges. I told you we should have told her to take oil," she said to Joyce.

"I didn't have any problem with the hinges," I said.

"But you said you saw the fabric, didn't you?" Minnie interrupted. "The Harris tweed. Nice, wasn't it?"

"It could have been," I agreed, "if it wasn't singed. That's what I'm trying to tell you. The cottage burned. To the ground. If your fabric was there, it isn't anymore."

"That can't be right," Minnie said. "It's too early for wood stoves."

"Remember last year?" Bernadette reminded her. "We had a cold snap."

"You didn't get our fabric?" Joyce persisted.

"There was a fire," I repeated. "Someone died. Smoke inhalation. In their sleep."

"Who?" Bernadette asked. Peaceful deaths were to be mourned less. "Anyone we know?"

"Must have been the renter," Minnie interrupted. "The ghostbuster."

My head hurt. "The ghostbuster?" I asked. Did everyone know Twyla the medium but me?

"Yes. The lady from the city. The one who claimed she could commune with lost sailors. She stayed here and there up and down the coast. But only in old houses, near the water." Bernadette lifted the lid of the teapot and peered in. Satisfied, she refilled her cup. "She made little movies about it."

"Reels," Minnie corrected. "My granddaughter explained it to me. She called the lady a social media spiritual influencer."

"There must have been some money in it," Bernadette noted. "No offense to the cottage, Valerie, but that lady stayed in some pretty fancy places. Summer homes, on the ocean."

"She was an amateur," Joyce sniffed. "I don't care where she stayed. You don't go to ghosts, they come to you. Poor soul, she'll find all that out soon enough."

"What goes around comes around," Minnie added, as if this made sense. "Back to the fabric. So, we don't know where it is. Maybe it burned up, but probably it didn't. The fire must be to cover up that someone took it."

"I bet that's it, Min," Bernadette agreed. "You can't trust thieves."

"That's highly valuable merchandise," Joyce said. "There's only one thing to do. Wait for the next move. It will come the usual way. Probably tomorrow."

"What will come?" I asked. My head hurt. I should have stayed home.

The three women looked at me, amazed at my naïveté.

"The mail," Minnie explained. "That's how they'll send it."

"Send what?" I asked, sagging in surrender.

"The ransom note. What we have to pay to get it back." Joyce folded her napkin, signaling that tea was done. I had failed in my mission; she'd take it from here. "We'll let you know when it arrives."

On the road home from Seaview Manor, a familiar RCMP cruiser passed me. Wade Corkum was at the wheel. Next to him, in plain clothes, was someone I knew well.

Chester. My kid who was supposed to be at work nearly a thousand miles away. My child who didn't know how to use a phone.

I nearly drove into the ditch.

What was Chester doing here in Gasper's Cove? Why hadn't he waved at me when they passed? Why didn't he tell me he would be here? Why wasn't he answering his phone? And more to the point, what was he doing in an RCMP vehicle? I straightened my car on the highway and flashed my lights. The occupants of the cruiser ignored me.

This was no way to treat a mother. This was no way to treat me. My patience was long gone, and my resources were depleted. I would find out what was going on. I stepped on the gas, propelled by indignation. At the bottom of the hill, instead of making the turn onto the causeway and to the RCMP detachment on the Drummond side as I expected, the cruiser kept going, down to the wharf, to Front Street, and to our store. I arrived just in time to see Wade and Chester disappear inside.

The fire. That had to be it. Wade had contacted Chester before I could, and they had come to tell me. I pulled up behind the cruiser and parked with one of my front wheels on the curb. I didn't care. I jumped out of the car, slammed the door closed, and crashed into the store.

Chester and Wade Corkum were talking to Colleen at the front counter. Toby was next to them, his big tail wagging so hard, it knocked the postcards out of the revolving rack.

Colleen saw me and the look on my face. "Officer Corkum is telling me about the cottage. I'm so, so sorry. A terrible thing to happen to your family. How are you doing?"

Not well, I thought. I looked at my middle son, and my eyes filled. Only a few months ago, I had helped him clean the cottage up before his brother and sister arrived. I'd brought him furniture, dishes, blankets, and curtains of my own. I reached down to pat Toby, so no one would see me blink away my tears. Chester reached over and wrapped his arms around me.

"It's okay, Mom," he said. "Me and Wade have already been out there. I wanted to see it before I talked to you. It's tough, but there's nothing we can do now."

"You were there? Already?" I asked, stepping back to look at my son. "What do you mean? You got here so soon. Why didn't you tell me you were coming? Why didn't you answer your phone?"

"Whoa, Momma. One at a time." Chester exchanged a look with Wade. They knew something I didn't. "I'm not working. I came to see Wade and you."

"You came to see Wade?"

"Yes, Mom. I flew into Nova Scotia yesterday morning. Wade picked me up and took me to Rollie's since our place was …" He swallowed. "… Rented. He came by today and told me about the fire. So, we went by to have a look. That's it."

I stared at my son. Who gets a ride to Gasper's with RCMP and not their own mother? Why was he staying with my cousin Rollie at his bed-and-breakfast and not with me? There was more to this story. I felt my nostrils flare and my blood pressure go up.

Wade stepped between Chester and me. "That fire, Valerie. It looked pretty bad. There was a fatality. CJ has been helpful. He helped me with the details. I understand a woman was renting the place. The investigator's on his way. He'll want that information."

"Investigator?" I asked Wade. "Aren't you going to find out what happened?"

"Actually, in the case of a fire, we don't usually get involved. Not unless there is a reason, some evidence of criminal intent. And usually, there isn't." Wade looked uneasily over at Colleen. She was picking up the postcards from the floor, her back to us, pretending she wasn't hanging onto every word, making sure she would be able to pass it all on accurately throughout the community. "Fire investigations are usually handled by the insurance company," Wade explained.

"That surprises me," I said. "Just as long as someone figures out what happened. We lost everything, but that poor woman died. And you," I said to my son, "still didn't tell me why you came down early."

"Maybe we can talk about this later," Chester said to placate me. "When things settle down."

There was no chance of that. "Tell me now."

Chester looked to Toby for support. "I've got an interview coming up. Wade is helping me get ready for it." Chester paused. "But, Mom, this is not the time."

I ignored him. "Interview? What interview?"

"I'm thinking of a new job. A different career." Chester kept his voice light, but I knew he was reading my reaction. "I'm not happy where I am. I'm going to join the RCMP. That's what the interview is for. It's what I want to do."

"A Mountie? Are you crazy?" I stared at Wade, "No offense. But Chester, all that time in university? All that money? I thought you liked banking. You got the math prize in Grade Eleven. What about that?"

My son shifted uneasily and stared silently at the ancient boards on the floor, as if seeking their guidance.

Wade intervened. As the one in the uniform my son wanted to wear, which I had just insulted, he seemed to feel it was his responsibility to fill in the blanks. "We talked it over this winter," he explained, "after hockey. We discussed our jobs."

"Wade liked his. I didn't like mine," Chester took over, regaining his ground. "Look. You didn't make a fuss when Kay went to Scotland to learn to be a better vet. Because it was about animals, it was okay. And Paul, he's the baby, he can do whatever he wants. No one thought he'd last in law school, so vegan matcha bagels or whatever he's doing this week seems to be fine with you. But me? I've always been the boring one, your steady, good-with-money middle child. You know what you used to say to me, Mom? That I was the one who never caused you any trouble." My son glared at me, and I didn't blame him. I'd said exactly that.

"I'm sorry," I said, "so you're telling me ..."

I didn't get to finish my sentence.

"I don't want to work in finance anymore," Chester said, "being what everyone expected. I am going to be a Mountie."

"It's a great career," Wade volunteered. "Look at me."

I looked at Wade, this bald, ex-hockey player Chester told things to that he didn't tell me.

Behind me, someone cleared their throat.

I turned to see an older man with his glasses high on his comb-overed head and a thick builder's pencil behind one ear.

"Excuse me," he asked tentatively, taking two steps back. He had the air of a seasoned husband, aware there was emotion in the air and no desire to approach it. "Toilet gaskets?"

"Aisle three," I said, more abruptly than was polite.

The poor man nodded, then scurried off to the safety of the plumbing department.

We watched him go, and as soon as we were alone again, Chester held up his palms.

"Mom, before you say anything, let me explain. I spend all my time in a cubicle, looking at financial plans for people who have so much money, they shouldn't care what happens to it." He narrowed his eyes, taking aim with the accuracy of an offspring who knew his parent well. "Would you want to keep doing that? All day, every day?"

We both knew the answer.

I gave up. "What happens now?" I said.

"I've got some time off. I think I'll stick around for a while. Get ready for the interview, maybe ride with Wade a bit. Get a feel for the job."

"And you'll stay with Rollie?" I asked. My spare room was always ready.

"Rollie offered, and he said he could use some help out there with some jobs he's got going on." Chester shrugged. "I've got some time."

I reached down and put my hand on Toby's soft head. He would always need me. But Rollie was my first cousin, so at least Chester would be with family.

"Got it. Good idea," I said, as if I meant it. "You know where I am."

Chester seemed relieved that this was all I had to say. "I sure do. I'll call you later. Me and Wade got to go and follow up on some vandalism. " He reached over and hugged me. "Thanks for understanding, Momma. It means a lot."

And with that, he left.

CHAPTER SEVEN

When the door closed behind Wade and Chester, I looked at Colleen's sympathetic face. I wanted her to tell me that everything would be okay, that nothing worse would happen. But before she could do that, we were interrupted by the sound of loud banging and shouting overhead.

"Take that, you maniacs!" a shrill voice carried down the stairs. "The cat and I know you're up there. This is war."

Beside me, Toby froze, his head down so he could listen. Then, as if confirming some doggy suspicion, he made up his mind and ran off up the stairs. Colleen and I followed.

There, on the second floor, in the beautiful space we had renovated to sell local crafts, we found a tiny woman smashing a broom against the store's old, pressed metal ceiling.

I pried the broom from Muriel Hirtle's hand.

"What's going on?" I asked. Muriel was married to Tommy, the fisherman I'd seen only yesterday at the fire. She was usually not violent. Good quilters seldom are. By contrast, on the counter beside her, Shadow swayed her tail menacingly, her yellow eyes narrowed and fixated on something above her in the ceiling.

"It's the raccoons!" Muriel shouted. Shadow looked on like some feline supervisor. "They're back. Up there. Moving in for the winter."

"Raccoons?" I asked. "How do you know?" Raccoons were nocturnal and not likely to be making noises in the attic, if they were there, during the day.

"Shadow's been fussy. And I knew it. I could smell them," Muriel muttered, like some medieval witch. "Sure, they wash their hands like people, but nothing smells like a raccoon. So, I started knocking on the ceiling. And sure enough, I heard them, running around up there. Laughing."

"Sounds like them," Colleen agreed. "Raccoons have no sense of boundaries. They'd be looking to come in for a nice place to relax for the winter. Happens all the time."

"You got to get rid of them," Muriel insisted. "They'll tear up the insulation, eat up the wiring, chew up the framing. Next thing you know, the whole roof will collapse. And they couldn't care less. That's the thing about raccoons. They don't care."

Colleen crossed her arms over her purple floral top. There were tiny sequins arranged around the neckline. The women on that side of the family didn't like to let themselves go. "That's right. Raccoons will make holes in the drywall. Stick out their pointy noses and sneaky bandit eyes to look around for something to eat, or just to fool around." She picked up a cloth bag of maple syrup fudge, eyed the bars of hand-milled lavender soap, and considered some vanilla candles. "They'd have a real party in this place."

"So, what do I do?" I asked. I needed the roof of the store to stay where it was. Then, I remembered something Harry had said. "Muriel, does Tommy still do a little raccoon removing?"

"That he does," Muriel answered. "He'll help you out. By the way, he told me about the fire at the cottage. You have enough trouble without raccoons."

She wasn't wrong about that. "Would he have the time to get here quick and get them out?" I asked. "I know he has his boat and the fire department." I tried to move past the image of the tragic fire where I'd seen Tommy last.

"He's got more than enough time," Muriel said. "How many fires are there on a coast like this? And he does not feel welcome at the yacht club anymore with this new manager. These days, since he retired, he mostly sits at home, waiting for me to make him lunch, worrying about money." She leaned in. "He's even started to come with me when I turn over the summer places. That man doesn't know one end of the vacuum from another. I had to boot him out. I got my system. My technology," she held up a cell phone. "Owners send me the address, the dates I go in, wash the sheets and towels, do the floors, bathrooms, and kitchens, and I'm out. You know that. I used to do the same at the cottage." She sighed at the memory. "I move pretty fast for an old girl when there's no one else trailing behind me. The raccoons will keep Tommy out of my hair." She looked up at the ceiling. "He'll bring his secret weapon."

"What's that?" Bernadette asked.

"Classical music." Muriel explained, "Tommy brings in a couple of transistors and turns up the CBC. The Canadian Broadcasting Corporation. Raccoons hear that, and they'll go off, screaming into the night. Guaranteed." She looked up at the ceiling and called out to the invisible vermin, "Your days are numbered."

I wasn't sure, but I thought Shadow smiled.

I left the store with Colleen back at the counter on the first floor. Muriel and Shadow remained upstairs to check the perimeter of the Co-op for possible raccoon points of entry. With the store settled, I decided it was time to see Darlene. So, I drove home, left the car, clipped on Toby's leash, and headed off in the direction of Darlene's house on Flying Cloud Drive. Toby and I were halfway up there when we ran into the municipality's mayor pushing a small screened-in stroller down the street. Elliot Clark wore his usual pressed button-down white Oxford cloth shirt, but since it was nearing the end of the day, he had tucked it tightly into a pair of stonewashed jeans.

"Elliot," I called out, slowing Toby down so I could talk. "We don't often see you this side of the causeway. Don't you live over in Drummond?"

"I do," he said, "but I'm house-sitting over here for my executive assistant. She's visiting grandchildren in Newfoundland. Precious here"—he pointed to a large tabby inside the pet stroller—"likes her turn around the block."

"That's nice of you," I said, surprised to learn that the officious Elliot was also a cat sitter, though Precious seemed unimpressed by the arrangement. She glared at me from her little enclosure, noted I was with a big dog, and turned her head away.

"Oh, I don't mind," Elliot said, as close to gracious as I'd ever heard him. "Competent assistants are hard to keep. Nothing better than a good one. Nothing worse than one you can't trust." He adjusted the arms of his mirrored wrap-around sunglasses over his gray brush cut. "And besides, over here, I am closer to the yacht club. This time of year, it makes it easier to get in an evening sail."

"Right. The yacht club," I said. "I was talking to Harry. He told me you have a new manager." Diplomatically, I left out the part of Harry's report that involved the removal, under new management, of Elliot's commodore's parking space and the buoy for his boat.

"Oh, yes. Peter Tucker." Elliot clamped his thin lips together and gave me a moment to watch his blood pressure climb well above the recommended guidelines. "I thought I'd seen the last of him when I left the provincial government. We worked together."

Toby tugged at the leash for me to keep walking, but I stayed where I was. This was interesting. "I didn't know you knew him," I said. "I haven't met Peter myself. What's he like?"

"How would I describe him?" Elliot looked over at some boys playing stick hockey on the road, getting ready for the season. "He started as a lawyer. They brought him in to do forms and procedures, but he spent most of his time looking for errors in everyone else's work. I think everyone was happy when the zombies ended his career."

Elliot began rocking Precious in her stroller back and forth, as a mother would to try to settle down a fussy baby, but perhaps to soothe himself. Toby sat at my feet, watching them, his head swinging back and forth like a pendulum on a wall clock.

"Zombies?" The Nova Scotia civil service was more interesting than I thought. "What zombies?"

"You haven't heard of them?" Elliot looked at me with surprise. "Zombies are old laws left on the books but never enforced because they were struck down by the courts years ago. Peter became obsessed with them. He stopped doing his real job and spent all his time writing Ottawa and raging at them to take all zombies out of the federal Criminal Code. He called these statutes insults to the integrity of governance. Except, the only one who was insulted was him. No one else cared. You know Ottawa. They don't get too worked up about anything. They just want to be left alone."

I took Elliot's word for it. I didn't have much to do with the nation's capital. But as an ordinary citizen, I had questions.

"I don't understand," I said. "If something is a law but never used, why have it?"

Elliot sighed, as if this was not the first time he had had to explain this to the legalistically ignorant. "Look, there are two kinds of redundant laws. First, there are the damaging ones. The Treasure Trove Act passed in the 1950s is an example of that. It granted licenses to anyone who wanted to look for shipwrecks. After all, there are 10,000 off the Nova Scotia coast. I think the government at the time thought, why not? But those licenses let anyone take away 90 percent of the artifacts they find and just give 10 percent to the province. No other jurisdiction in North America was that dumb. That law was struck down in 2010. Zombies, on the other hand, are harmless legal clutter. Laws for activities no one would be charged for these days."

"What are examples?" I asked.

Elliot shrugged. "Dueling. Writing crime comics. Jumping out of a plane without a parachute—that was a big one. Paying for something with too much loose change. Pretending to practice witchcraft. Water-skiing at night. There are a bunch of them. But the fact that the government let this legislation stay on the books made Peter crazy. And let me tell you, there's a saturation level for crazy even in public service. You got to keep under it the limit. Peter went over it, so he got slid right out of government. Rumor was that someone he worked with got into his emails, made copies, and sent them up the chain. It was an embarrassment. So, he was retired off early and decided to come here. Why, I don't know. Maybe to just drive the locals nuts."

Briefly, I wondered if Elliot was aware of the parallels between his own story and Peter's. Both men had transplanted themselves to Gasper's Cove with civil service pensions and were trying to get us all organized.

Precious rolled in her stroller. This visit was taking too long. Elliot whispered an apology to her and, nodding goodbye, marched away.

I was about to do the same when my phone beeped in my pocket. I pulled it out.

Darlene.

Mom said you wanted to talk to me. U coming over?

Yes.

I tapped back.

What above? About?

Darlene always misspelled under pressure. Something was up.

You tell me.

I answered.

Darlene loved her emojis.

We are on our way.

I saw Darlene standing at her kitchen window when Toby and I got closer to her house. Then, she disappeared from view, and the side door opened. Once we were inside, Toby rushed ahead to eye the counter and the plate of baklava sitting there, a donation, provided no doubt by Sophia Kosoulas, Darlene's soon-to-be mother-in-law. I shooed my dog away and then sat on a kitchen chair. Darlene poured me a tea and handed me the mug. I waited until she sat down and pushed a plate with a baklava and a fork toward me before I went to work.

"Okay. What's up?" I asked. "Your mother's worried." I noticed that the turquoise gel nails around Darlene's tightly held cup needed to be redone. Darlene must be under huge stress if she would let a detail like that slip. I felt like I was drinking tea with a hairdresser deputy mayor version of a coiled spring.

I put my hand on Darlene's arm. "Talk to me."

"The wedding arrangements." A shadow flitted across Darlene's face. She tried to laugh it away. "The good thing about marrying a guy whose family owns a Greek restaurant is that the reception and food are all covered. But there's other stuff."

"Like what?"

"George wants this wedding to take," she said. "Be the only one that matters."

Underneath the table, Toby went still. He was listening, and I knew we were both thinking the same thing. George had been married once before, Darlene, three times.

"It will," I said. "This is the guy you should have married years ago."

"Yes," Darlene agreed. "No one knows that better than I do. And that's exactly why George wants this time to be more ... serious." She put down her fork, the pastry untouched. "He wants to do it in the church, the Greek Orthodox one in Halifax. I'm going to convert."

I relaxed. How hard could that be? I'd been to a Greek wedding once. I remembered a beautiful church and incense. Afterward, we danced all night. "That's great news," I said. "The bride and groom wear crowns during the ceremony. You'll like that."

"I know," Darlene said. "I do a nice updo, but that's not what's worrying me. I've got to see the priest."

"What's the problem with that?"

"My marital history is, what would you call it?" Darlene asked. "Not the best. What if he doesn't like me? What if they don't take me? What if I blow the intake meeting? What will I say to George?"

"Look," I said. "This is how this is going to work. You make the appointment, and I'll go to Halifax with you. Chester is here. He can take care of Toby. Don't worry. This priest will love you. You'll get in."

"Would you do that for me?" Darlene's eyes were wide, blue, and worried. She hadn't been this way for any of her other weddings, and I'd stood for her at all of them. "And maybe, if you come, we can look around and get ideas."

"Ideas?"

"For my dress, the one I want you to make for me," she said. "My grandmother says she has a surprise. Something she put away."

I choked on my tea. I had to have a chat with Bernadette. But that would have to wait. First, I'd go to Halifax and give the Greek Orthodox Church a chance to snap up Darlene.

CHAPTER EIGHT

First thing Monday morning, Darlene and I headed to Halifax. The trip took longer than we planned. More than once, we had to stop and wait because of construction. The Nova Scotia road-building season was nearly over. Crews had been busy up and down the coast, blasting rock and widening the highways to make room for the increase in tourist traffic, and they were still at it. Once, we passed Alex Flynn, the volunteer firefighter's survey van. We waved, but I didn't think he saw us.

Despite the slow going, we made good use of the time. George's mother, Sophia, had given us questions and answers to rehearse on our way. Darlene had even brought a copy of our old high school yearbook with its picture of her and George at the graduation dance. I felt if the priest was at all a romantic, Darlene would be fine.

After I dropped Darlene off at the church on the Northwest Arm for her meeting, I decided to go to a Guy Frenchy's, the local resale chain, to pass the time. It was Darlene who had gotten me into thrifting. She was a master at it, her fingers adept at flicking through the racks, always able to find treasures I would have missed. Once, she found a Pringles of Scotland sweater, shrunken stiff, but otherwise perfect. I'd made it into felted mitts. Another time, she'd snapped up a raw silk jacket. I'd relined it, and she'd worn it to be sworn in as deputy mayor. Today, I decided I'd look for silk ties to make into piping.

The store was busy. As soon as I was through the doors, I saw armies of dedicated mothers and grandmothers around each big wooden table, heads down as they worked systematically through piles of clothes for babies, boys, girls, and ladies. Not wanting to compete, I found three ties in the men's section, two striped and one a deep maroon. I made my way to the counter to pay. As I stood in line, I looked around and noticed a tower of bundles stacked up near the double doors at the front of the store. The sign above them read:

RAGS

BALBRIGGAN 25 LBS. $25.00 #103
(Best Seller most used rags)
Cotton T-shirt/thermal material.
*Ideal for auto shops, electrical, industrial
suppliers, and maintenance contractors.*

WHITE BALBRIGGAN 25 LBS. $35.00 #106
White cotton T-shirt. Best grade of white.
*Ideal for polishing, staining, and any application
where softeners and purity are essential.*

I worked my way down the list to the not-so-best-sellers, half-pound bags. Virtually lint-free. Excellent for polishing, staining, and glass-cleaning applications.

Curious, I moved in for a closer look. Fabric was always interesting.

And this fabric certainly was.

The lint-free white fabric was, in fact, Swiss dot cotton. I was sure of it. The crumpled knot next to it was silk organza interfacing. I'd know it anywhere. And that wasn't any old cotton flannel at the bottom of the bag. It was, I knew in my bones, vintage cotton/wool Viyella, the kind loomed in Nottingham, England, since 1784. The only fabric missing was the Harris tweed.

I pushed my way through the line until I could grab one of the half-pound bags. I held it up close and tried to feel the texture through the plastic. Was this what I thought it was? Genuine Harris tweed? It was.

I drew in a big breath of disinfected, secondhand air.

"Manager," I called out. "I want to see the manager. Now."

She was half my age and didn't know fabric. However, the manager knew customers: which ones were easy, which ones were trouble, and which ones were crazy. She looked me up and down and put me in the last category.

"Those are rags," she said slowly. "Just old cloth. For cleaning."

I cringed at the word *cloth*.

"Can you open the bags, please, so I can look?" I asked her, scanning the clientele. Someone here must have a lighter. I would do the burn test to make my point. Natural fibers, like silk, cotton, and wool, left an ash. Synthetics rolled into melted balls. "All we need is a match, and we can take a flame to it. That's high-quality fabric in those bags."

"Flame?" The manager raised her pierced eyebrows. "I am afraid we can't do that. People drop off old cloth, and we chop it up. If you want any of it, buy a bag."

"Chop it up? You're kidding."

"No, I'm not," said this person who didn't know any better. "If the cloth comes in a big piece, we cut it up into rag sizes. Any in particular you want? They go fast, these rags. The garages love them."

I hardly heard her. My mind was moving too fast. "Where do they come from?" I asked. "Your donations."

"Anywhere," the manager said. "We've got bins behind every store."

"But if you want to trace it back to the point of origin? To who dropped it off," I persisted, "can you do that?"

The young manager laughed. "No way. Most things are dumped in the bins after hours. That's all I can tell you."

I knew what I had to do. I pulled my credit card out of my wallet. "I'll take four bags please," I said. "The one with the white fabric and three of the smaller ones."

The manager smiled. "Good choice." She took my card. "Your husband a mechanic?"

"No," I said. "He's not."

Darlene bounced over to the car and got in. Clearly, converting to the Greek Orthodox Church agreed with her.

"Done," she said. "Couple of things, George and I have to come back, but I'm in. Under the wire."

"What do you mean?" I asked.

"There's a limit to how many previous marriages you can have to get married in the Orthodox Church. Three. But those have to be ones that were performed in the church. But since my previous marriages were civil, they don't count," Darlene beamed at me. "I got in on a technicality. I already called George—he's thrilled."

Only Darlene, I thought, would be in this situation. "How was the priest?" I asked her.

"Lovely man. Couldn't be nicer," she said. "And you were right about the crowns you wear at the ceremony. For the first time ever, I actually feel like a bride." She reached down under her seat for a lever. "Hey, why is my seat so far forward?"

"Sorry about that," I said, pulling away from the church and onto the main road. "I got some bags at Frenchy's. They're in the back seat."

Darlene twisted around to look. "What? Cleaning rags?" she asked. "You've decided to become a different person? One who likes housework?"

"Please. I clean my house. The parts that I notice," I said. "Often. But that's not why I bought those bags. You're not going to believe it ..."

Darlene interrupted me—she wasn't listening. "You know, I keep telling you to get a cleaning lady if you don't like to do it yourself. Why don't you ask Miriam Hirtle? Nothing makes a good impression like a sparkling sink and stove."

I rolled my eyes at the spruce trees as we sped our way out of the city and onto the highway home to Gasper's Cove. I'd seen Darlene clean the vent on the back of her fridge with cotton swabs; I had no idea when I had last looked behind my own fridge. This year? This decade?

"My house is clean enough for me and Toby. For family," I said, "and friends tell me the day before they are coming. That's not what I want to talk about." My voice was too loud in the small interior of my car, but I had news. "I think there is fabric in those bags—not rags, but real fabric. From our cottage, before it burned down."

I had Darlene's attention. Her head whipped around to look at the back seat again. "Doesn't look burnt to me," she said. "What are you talking about?"

So, I told her, leaving out the fact that her own grandmother and her friends were thieves. "There was some good fabric stored in the cottage. Everything went in that fire; there wasn't anything left. The fabric should have gone too. But I found at least some of it at Frenchy's." I looked sideways at Darlene to see if she was following me. "That means the fabric was removed from the cottage before the fire. Taken and donated. Which makes no sense."

"Of course it makes sense," Darlene said. "I'm sure the previous owners got rid of a lot of old junk when they moved in."

"I don't think it was the previous owners. I found it in Halifax. They would have dropped stuff off in Gasper's Cove. Plus, none of them knew the fabric was there. It was hidden in a secret hiding place."

"What hiding place?" Darlene asked. "Put there by who?"

"The rumrunner who built the cottage put in a secret compartment behind a shelf." I was getting in deep. "Some people knew about the hiding place. That's where they stashed the fabric."

I could feel Darlene's stare. I kept my eyes on the road.

"But why bother putting it anywhere? It was just fabric. And are you saying these fabric-hiding people went back to the cottage, dug it out, and then drove down to Halifax to drop it off at Frenchy's ? And you came up with this crazy theory when you were looking for secondhand clothes while I was becoming Greek Orthodox?" Darlene shook her head. "Boy, this has been some productive trip."

"I know," I agreed, "except the people who hid the fabric couldn't be the same ones who went and got it."

"How do you know that?" Darlene asked. "Who told you all this anyway? Someone who knew this rumrunner?"

"No, he's long gone," I replied. "Just a ghost now. I wonder if that poor woman who was staying at the cottage was trying to talk to him. I don't think she got through." I thought about Twyla and her spiritual attempts. "Not to speak ill of the dead, but I think she was a bit of a flake."

Darlene unzipped her bag, pulled out a bag of potato chips, and spoke to the scenery flying past the window.

"She's not the only one," she said.

CHAPTER NINE

Back on Gasper's Island, I dropped Darlene off at the Agapi. I knew Sophia would want a full report. Now that Darlene had seen the priest, the real planning could begin.

As I watched her walk through the doors of the restaurant, I was ashamed that I felt abandoned. I knew why. Since my return to Gasper's Cove, Darlene and I had been a team, two middle-age single women making, for the first time, lives of their own. How much would that change when she was married? Everyone was moving on. Even my former husband had resettled, with his second (or was it third?) Pilates instructor. I didn't like change. Was that a mistake?

I decided to keep driving, I decided to see Stuart.

I didn't know why. Then, I did.

Stuart would know what to do about my discovery at Frenchy's. He was calm, reasonable, and reliable. And when it mattered, on my side. I'd show him the fabric. I'd tell him the story, leaving out who it was about.

I crossed the causeway and drove into Drummond and parked in front of Stuart's office. My head was deep in one of the bags in my back seat, digging for a sample to show, when I felt a finger twist into my shoulder. I jumped and smacked my head on the metal door frame. I backed out of the car. I straightened up. Then, I nearly fell over.

There he was, the last person I'd expected to see. The long-gone and never missed Creepy Kevin, Darlene's second husband. Kevin Johnson, breaker of hearts, emptier of bank accounts, king of conflicts. The last time I had seen him was when Colleen and I had dumped him at the Acadian Lines bus station on the far side of Drummond. At that time, he'd been one step ahead of the lawyers. We'd assumed we'd never see him again.

And now, he was back.

"There I was, walking down the street, and I said to myself, Valerie Rankin, I'd recognize that backside anywhere." Kevin jabbed me, this time in my shoulder. "Aren't you a sight for sore eyes?"

I didn't respond, but that didn't mean I wasn't thinking. I was doing a mental inventory of the contents of my car and my purse, hoping I had a sharp instrument like a seam ripper handy. "What are you doing here?" I asked.

"Business," Kevin ran his hand over his gelled hair, a flatter, deeper black than I remembered. He and his aftershave moved in close to me, and he winked. "Strictly business, although I might take a run over the causeway and see my lovely ex-wife." Kevin widened his small ferret eyes, tilted his head, and paused, looking for female sympathy. It was a maneuver I had seen more times than I cared to count. "Biggest mistake of my life that I let the love of my life slip away." He sighed, watching me to see if I felt his pain.

Slip away? What was he talking about?

More like we all booted him out.

"What kind of business?" I asked, changing the subject. "With who?" Steady employment had never been Kevin's specialty.

"Working with my dad," he said. Kevin's father owned a successful insurance company that, so far, had escaped having to employ his son. "I was in seeing my old buddy Stu," he added, tossing his shiny head in the direction of the Chinese restaurant located just under S.J. Campbell Engineering Limited. "Stu was a big help. Always is." Kevin reached over to tap the end of my nose, but I pulled back.

Kevin snorted. If I was immune to his charm, it was my loss. "I'll be here for a while," he said, turning to walk away. "See you around. Be like old home week, back in Last Gasp, just like I never left."

I watched Kevin go until I couldn't stand it anymore. "Darlene is getting married," I called out to the departing back of the most annoying man in Canada. "She's real happy."

Kevin's strut slowed for a minute, then he shrugged, shook it off, and kept walking.

I wasn't sure if he had heard me or if he just didn't care.

I slammed my car door and tried to settle down. Kevin Johnson had broken Darlene's heart, many times. Making trouble was something Kevin did recreationally. His reappearance was not a good thing. It never was.

Why was he here?

I had to find out.

I headed for the door Kevin had exited and charged up the stairs. When I arrived at the second floor, I went past the dentist's and pushed the door to Stuart's office open so hard it hit the wall and its smoked glass vibrated. The waiting room was empty, and with no receptionist to stop me, I walked into the inner office without knocking.

Stuart Campbell, Gasper's Cove and Drummond's most experienced civil engineer, was hard at work. He had tweezers in one hand and a bottle of wood glue in the other. He appeared to be engaged in critical repairs to the jibboom of the miniature *Bluenose II* schooner he kept on his desk.

He stopped whistling when he saw me. "Hi," he said. "Am I supposed to be somewhere, doing something?"

"Happy to see you too," I answered. Stuart put down his tweezers and glue and looked at me, his blue eyes clear and innocent. It occurred to me then that the most attractive men are the ones who don't know it, but I kicked that thought aside.

"What are you doing talking to Creepy Kevin?" I demanded. "You should know better."

Stuart didn't react. He was getting good at not reacting to me. I'd analyze that later.

"Excuse me," he said. "It was a professional meeting." He picked up a business card from his desk and pushed it over to me.

I picked it up and read.

KEVIN JOHNSON

Johnson's has you covered.

My fingers let the card fall back onto the desk. "Don't be impressed," I said. "That's not his company. Don't believe anything he tells you. He's not to be trusted."

Stuart leaned back in his swiveling office chair and put his fingers together like a steeple. My father used to do the same thing. "That's a pretty drastic assessment," he said. "What do you have against this guy? He seemed nice enough."

I plopped myself down in Stuart's visitor's chair.

"Kevin Johnson was Darlene's second husband," I began. "The one between the guy she married out of high school who turned out to be a drinker and number three, the bus driver she married on the rebound."

"As in rebound from Kevin?" Stuart said. His face went serious. He liked Darlene.

"Yes. He was one smooth character in the day, or at least that's what we thought. He was the kind of guy who seemed sophisticated if you grew up in a small town. He had a foreign car, he drank Campari. He told Darlene he loved her on the first date." Uncomfortable memories were returning, things I had never told Stuart. "He came to the house and brought her mom flowers." That wasn't all he brought, I remembered—there was also a friend.

Stuart was quiet, as if he knew what was coming next. "So, what happened?"

"We all thought she'd hit the jackpot. They got married. I was her bridesmaid." Just like she had been mine. "But Kevin was a liar, a cheat. He even tried to hustle me the night of the rehearsal." I'd tried to tell her, but she hadn't listened. It was too late. For the both of us.

"Oh, hell." Stuart sighed and looked out the window at the water. "How long did it last?"

"Not that long," I said. There was no way around it—I had to tell him what had happened to me too. "She didn't hang in as long as I did." I saw the question in Stuart's face. "You see, I married his best friend. I had children, she didn't, so I didn't want to believe it."

"Believe what?"

"Creepy Kevin and my ex covered up for each other." I took a big breath. This was hard. "They cheated on us and lied about it. To both of us."

"Man, I'm sorry," Stuart reached over and squeezed my hand. "No wonder you were upset he was here." He pulled his hand away and looked uncomfortable. "He's investigating a claim."

"What claim?" I asked. Then, I knew. "Not our cottage, not the fire? They'll cover it. That's why we have insurance. They have to."

"Well, not immediately," Stuart hesitated. "Insurance companies investigate first."

I opened my mouth to protest, but Stuart held up a hand.

"Let me finish," he said and reached over and delicately placed the *Bluenose* back on her perch. "Johnson has to look at all options, including any that would void the claim."

"What options?" I asked. I started to feel sick: The only way that family cottage could be rebuilt was with insurance money.

"Arson, involving someone who would stand to gain." Stuart paused, waiting for this to sink in. "I'm afraid Kevin Johnson is going to be here for a while."

CHAPTER TEN

I stared at Stuart.

I didn't believe this.

I knew Kevin Johnson would bring trouble. I knew it. "But that doesn't explain why he was here."

"Look, I did the original inspection on the cottage before Chester bought it. Mold, water, electrical, structural. Like you would before any sale. Johnson wanted the drawings and the report." Stuart ignored my eye roll. "Part of his due diligence."

"So, what happens next?" I asked.

"Don't let yourself get worked up," Stuart said. "They always consider arson as part of any fire investigation. Johnson says it's usually hard to prove, but there are things about this one that he noticed."

"Like what?"

Stuart looked like he regretted starting this conversation. "Johnson told me fires usually start in one place, but the burn patterns in this one showed it began at three different points. Kevin's wondering if someone set the fire in a way to make sure it caught." Stuart pressed his mouth into a tight line, as if he was trying to hold his words in. "And there was the blue bag."

"Blue bag?" I asked.

"Yeah. Yesterday, the recycling truck came by. One of the guys on it saw there had been a fire. That made him remember a bag he'd picked up there last week. It had plastic jugs in it and smelled of gasoline. As a result, when he got back to the depot, he called it in. His manager got in touch with Kevin this morning."

I leaned into the chair's wicker back and tried to absorb this. "That's Kevin's evidence? He thinks our fire was lit because of recycling?" I looked at the framed drawings on the walls of Stuart's office. Most were technical drawings, specifications for boat builders, one an elaborate patent document of a boat hook, signed in elaborate cursive, *J. Jordan Inventor.* Stuart was a careful man; he wouldn't be telling me this if he wasn't taking it seriously himself. "Kevin is an idiot," I said, to dismiss and erase the whole idea. "Coincidence. The fire was an accident."

"I'm sure you're right," Stuart said. "You have to let this process play out."

There was something else. We both knew it.

"This isn't just about a building that burned down, is it?" I asked. "That poor woman died. This could turn into bigger trouble than arson. Am I right?"

"Possibly," Stuart admitted. "If the fire was deliberately set, the death would be considered manslaughter. But let's not get ahead of ourselves. Even Kevin admitted he would need more evidence before he could even make the call it was arson. It will take time, more tests, interviewing possible witnesses, things like that. Weeks, maybe a month, to get that all done."

"But Kevin has his suspicions, doesn't he?" I asked. "Involving my family?" I stood up. "I'm going. This is ridiculous."

Stuart came around his desk, close to me. "Valerie, wait. It will all work out. Take it easy."

"Take it easy?" Stuart reached for my arm. I took a step back. "Look. I'm not standing by and letting Creepy Kevin decide what happens. That's that. I'm going to find out what's going on."

"Wait." Stuart made a shushing sound that annoyed me. "Just wait."

"As if that's going to happen." I was vibrating with emotion, directed at Stuart, Kevin, and anyone else I could think of. "Don't you even think about trying to stop me," I added.

"I couldn't stop you if I tried," Stuart said. "Could I?"

At least we agreed on something. "No," I said. There was nothing else to say. I let the door slam on my way out.

I texted Chester as soon as I was back in my car.

Where are you?

There was a pause.

Just got to the beach, surfing.

Stay there. Don't go in the water. Be there soon.

Why?

Chester tapped back.
My nerves.

We have to talk.

???

I ignored Chester's last text. I was already on my way.
I knew exactly where to find him. The boys had started
to surf in their early teens and, like all locals, knew where
to find the best waves. But those beaches were no longer
private. In the fall hurricane season, surfers came in from
around the world for waves as high and fierce as any on
Earth. The parking lot beside the once-secluded cove was
almost full when I got there. Battered vans, wet towels
draped over the windows, alternated with RVs with out-
of-province plates and small cars with big boards strapped
onto the roofs. Beside one of those cars, I saw my son in his
wetsuit, the long zipper pull hanging down the back, his
face turned toward the small black shapes out in the water,
paddling toward a big break. When I pulled up beside him,
Chester reached over and opened my door.

"Yo, Momma. What's up?" Chester asked.

Where would I start? I looked at my son's handsome face,
shiny with Vaseline to protect his skin from the cold water.
He didn't look like he had a care in the world—at least, not
yet.

"Look. I've come from Stuart's. He tells me an insurance
investigator, someone Darlene and I used to know, is here
to check on the fire." I stopped for a reaction, but Chester
leaned against the hood of the car and waited, relaxed. "Did
you know about this? Why didn't you tell me?"

"Because it's not your problem? Mom, we own the cottage: me, Paul, and Kay. Dude had some routine questions." Chester eyed the ocean; this conversation was keeping him from a nice swell. "Mr. Johnson was just doing his job. Routine. What he should be doing." He paused. "Terrible about that woman. Really bad. I hope there is a thorough investigation. That's the right thing to do. And when that's done, and it is clear what caused the accident, we'll get the insurance money and start over."

"Stuart thinks there might be some trouble with the money," I said. If there was going to be bad news, it was up to me to tell it. "The investigator, Kevin, is looking for evidence that someone started the fire on purpose. And if he finds it, the insurance company won't pay out."

"Arson?" Chester looked as if this was news to him. "You mean someone deliberately burned our place down? Who? Why?"

"I don't know. But what if Kevin thinks our family was involved? I wouldn't put it past him." There, I'd said it. "I know that's crazy. You guys would only use the insurance money to rebuild. Your name is on the deed, but look at your job. All the security you have, your salary." I wanted to remind him of that.

I stopped and waited for Chester to respond. Instead, he pointed to a battered old picnic table askew on a sand dune.

"Mom, let's go sit down," Chester said. "There's something I have to tell you."

"What do you mean?" My feet slipped over the sand as I slid onto the rough bench of the table.

"Okay. This isn't about the cottage. I haven't told you everything."

I tried to stay steady on the sloping seat.

"That part about money ..." Chester's voice trailed off. "That situation is sort of fluid."

"Fluid?"

"I don't have that job at the bank in Toronto anymore."

"You quit?" This made no sense to me. "Because of this crazy RCMP idea? And you quit before you got accepted?" Chester was my sensible son. Maybe not.

"No," Chester said slowly, "I didn't exactly quit. We came to a 'mutual agreement to sever our business arrangement.'" He sighed. "I screwed up with a client. Capital gains."

"Capital what?" I asked. I was proud of my son, but I had no actual idea what he did.

"It has to do with taxes," Chester explained. "If a client makes a pile of money selling an investment—say, property or stocks—they pay tax on it. And the more money they make, the more tax they pay. One thing an investment advisor, like I was, does, is make sure that things are spread out, so the client doesn't get hit with paying an undue, or worse, an unexpected, amount of tax."

I tried to translate this into my own reality. I understood that anything that involved taxation was a worry. "So, you got fired because you made a capital whatever mistake with someone's tax?"

"More or less that's it," Chester admitted. "I was bored out of my mind. Most of my clients were loaded with conservative portfolios. I moved things around, bought and sold what I was supposed to, when I was supposed to, but I forgot to ask the right questions."

"Like what?"

"Like what else they had going on. I think I got numb with the routine of it." Chester's eyes were focused on the water, or maybe on a scene I couldn't share. "Ironically, one of my clients sold a cottage, an old one, for a huge amount. I was doing some trades on their behalf in that quarter, and with so much money coming in all at the same time, they got slammed with a big tax bill they weren't expecting. I felt awful. It made me realize I was the wrong guy for that job." Chester's face twisted with embarrassment. "I left. It was like a sign I had to be who I really was. I had been talking to Wade, and it got me thinking. I wanted work that matters. I never wanted anything before in my life. Not really wanted it. But I do this. That's why I came down, to go over my application with Wade, get ready for my intake assessment."

"Your next career is the least of your worries," I said. "You know how this will look don't you? Kevin will see an out-of-work young guy, and he'll figure you need money. What are we going to do?"

"We? Do? Mom, this isn't about you. If there's any questions, I'll deal with this Kevin guy. I have nothing to hide. Nothing. That's all that matters." Chester stood up and walked over to the surfboard he had strapped to the roof of the car. "You stay out of it. No getting involved, no interfering. Last thing I need."

There was something about his tone that reminded me of Stuart. Anything I did wasn't interfering. It was my job. I was his mother. I was worried. I was scared.

"But Chester, what's the plan?" I persisted.

He had the board down. "What does it look like? I'm going surfing." He bent down to gather the lead that would connect the board to his ankle. "Mom, all I want you to do is chill. Can you do that for me?"

"I'll try," I said. As if that was going to happen.

CHAPTER ELEVEN

After I left the beach, I didn't want to go home. I was too upset and too restless. I knew Kevin Johnson better than anyone. I remembered the letter he'd written to Darlene years ago, the one he'd asked me to pass on and I had never delivered. It had twisted the blame for his cheating back onto her, claiming she'd left him no choice. His arrival in Gasper's Cove was an omen, a memory of past pain, returned to bring trouble back to us.

I needed to talk to someone and wasn't sure who that was. I wasn't ready to tell Darlene that Kevin was here and ruin her peace. I'd overreacted in Stuart's office, but I wasn't quite ready to make amends. Chester was on the waves and had no more words for me. I wanted an ally and needed to talk to someone who would understand how I felt.

The car drove itself to Seaview Manor.

This time, the ladies were not out in front of the building or in the dining room having tea. Instead, I found them off to the side of the tiny lending library in the multipurpose recreation room. There they were at a table, facing the broad back of a man in a blue windbreaker. As I paused in the open doorway, Joyce waved at me.

"Hello dear," she said, in a sweet voice I hardly recognized. "Come to visit? We have a gentleman caller."

The man in the windbreaker turned around, annoyed by the interruption. I saw a Gasper's Cove Yacht Club logo on his jacket. Underneath it was embroidered the word *Manager*. This was the famous Peter Tupper. At last, I thought, we meet.

I wasn't impressed.

To be fair, I was not in my best mood, but something about the man's face annoyed me as soon as I saw it. In the split second while he appraised me and dismissed me, I recognized in it a kind of belligerence all too familiar to women. An invisible woman. Not young enough to be attractive and therefore too old to matter.

"We're not finished here. Do you mind?" he asked.

I saw a flash of something in Joyce's face come and go, to be replaced by a staged mask of elderly innocence. She was up to something. "But there are berries along that lane," she said, as if continuing some conversation. "Wild raspberries. What about the birds? The raccoons?"

I walked into the room and sat down on a chair on the side to watch whatever was going on.

"Birds? They can go anywhere." Peter said. From where I sat, I could see him roll his eyes. "Just sign the waiver so our members can use the path, cut it back, and get it paved for extra parking."

"But that way to the water has been used by my family since my great-granddad was a boy. That's why they named it ..." Minnie hesitated. "What do they call it?" She widened her eyes and looked to Bernadette for support.

"Grandfathered," Joyce answered instead. "It's as good as belongs to your family."

Peter stroked a dark pencil-thin mustache and pulled in his shoulders, as if gathering and trying to contain his patience. His large ears were red with annoyance. Something about him reminded me of Clark Gable—the handsome face, the ears. "I know that. The municipal planning office explained it. That's why all you have to do," he pushed a paper and pen a little closer to Minnie, "is sign this waiver. It's not as if you use that path yourself these days."

This was the wrong thing to say.

"I don't have my glasses. I think I wear glasses," Minnie said. "Who are you again?"

"I've already told you three times. Peter Tupper, from the yacht club."

"Who are your people?" Joyce asked. "Don't I know them?"

"Doubt it. We've gone over that too. I'm from Halifax. No family. Listen, I have things to do." Peter clicked the pen, as if getting it ready for action. "Sign the paper, and I'll be on my way."

"Tupper?" Joyce persisted. "There was a man once years ago, known in the community, ran for office. The Conservatives, or the Liberals?"

"Both, I think it was," Minnie said. "Casey Baldwin, the famous flier, the one who set up the big park in Cape Breton, came down to speak for him. Not that it did that Tupper any good," Minnie added, peering at Peter. "Are you that gentleman, come to get our votes? Do you look familiar?"

"Your glasses, Min," said Bernadette. "Did you check your knitting bag? That's a lovely pattern. Basket stitch, make a nice cardigan."

"Warm," Joyce agreed, "for the winter. I should make one when I finish my mitts. Putting cables on the back."

"That's nice. For the kids?" Bernadette asked. "Make them in threes. They'll lose one."

"Particularly the boys," Min said. "They'll leave them at school." She had another thought. "The dining room. Maybe that's where I left my glasses. Or maybe not."

"Oh, my goodness," Joyce said. "That blueberry crumble, last night, wasn't it good?"

"Not too dry," Bernadette agreed. "Those were good berries. Someone picked them when they were ripe."

"Nothing like a good *wild* berry," Joyce said. She looked at the visitor. "Why don't you stay for dinner? They might have some left over."

"Friday," Bernadette added. "Fish. They do a nice fish. Haddock. Is it Friday? Or Tuesday? I get them mixed up. Then, it would be chicken."

"Wednesday," Peter grunted and tried once again with Min. "Are you going to sign this or not?"

Minnie's lids fluttered and dropped, as if she was taking a nap. From where I sat, I saw her kick Joyce's foot.

"She gets tired," Joyce explained. "Basket stitch. The counting takes it out of you. Unless you write it down. I use old envelopes." She paused and regarded the visitor, as if she had just noticed him. "Who did you say you were again? Are you sure you're not from around here? Did you find Min's glasses?"

Peter stood up, the polyester poplin of his jacket snapping, the zipper making the sound of a row of dominoes falling, as he pulled it closed. Standing, he was shorter than I expected. But born burly and determined.

"This is useless. I'll have to go back to the council." He waited for the ladies to do something to spare him that trouble. Min started to snore, maybe a little too theatrically. Bernadette pulled a tissue from the sleeve of her sweater and hid her face in it. Joyce's facial muscles struggled to arrange themselves in the unaccustomed shape of simple passivity.

"Come and visit us again," she said. "It's been lovely to talk to someone in the Navy."

When Peter left, after a brief stop to complain to the woman stroking a gray cat at the front desk, the ladies relaxed.

"Navy?" Bernadette asked. "Where did that come from?"

"I improvised," Joyce said. "I was in the moment."

"Counting? Basket stitch? I'm insulted. Knit eight, purl eight, eight rows and reverse," Min said.

"I know," Joyce said. "But that line about the envelopes, I had to use it."

"You were right about the berries though," Min conceded. "Raccoons can strip a whole line of blueberries in one night if they work in teams."

"I mean the nerve of the man, grandfathered is grandfathered. Parking lot? Give me strength," Bernadette said. "Valerie, you look like you have something on your mind. What is it? I know you didn't come by to see us audition for the Academy Awards."

I reached over and straightened the chair Peter had vacated. "You're right. I have a lot on my mind. I'm full of worries, to tell you the truth."

"Talk to us." The real Joyce was back in charge. "We've seen and heard everything."

So, I did.

First, reluctantly, I told the ladies they were right—it looked like someone unknown had liberated their stolen fabric before the fire. And rather than try to sell it, they had dumped it in a donation box.

"Collateral damage," Joyce interrupted. "They were looking for something else and gathered up our fabric by mistake. No idea how valuable it was. That explains why we haven't had a ransom note." She tapped her palm to her forehead. "We should have thought of this possibility." She stopped and stared at me. "We have one clue, though. Whoever it was didn't know quality yardage."

Minnie was silent, then I noticed her eyes looked teary. "You're right, Joyce, but what a sin ... the Viyella, the Swiss dot ... I wanted to touch them one last time."

"Pull yourself together," Joyce ordered. "Valerie here says she has real trouble. We got to hear it all. We can do our mourning later."

"You're right," Minnie sniffed. "Sorry."

"So, what's wrong? Family trouble?" Bernadette asked. With a large clan of her own, most trouble, in her experience, led back to a relation.

Her intuition was not wrong.

"Chester, my son," I began. "He quit his good job at the bank and wants to join the RCMP." The ladies looked at each other. Desk jobs were safe. Anyone who handled money for a living was bound to do well. They understood how I felt. "He came back to Gasper's the day before the fire. His name is on the deed," I continued. "A woman died. The insurance investigator thinks it might be arson."

I took a breath and looked around the table. I saw that I didn't need to add two and two together for these women. They had lived one step ahead of disasters their whole lives. Most fishermen's wives did. They knew what I was saying. They knew why I was worried.

"But he's a nice boy," Minnie said to reassure me, but then her voice trailed off. Like us all, she knew from experience that it was the nicest people who often ended up in the most trouble.

"It gets worse," I said.

The table went still. This was hard to imagine.

"The man from the insurance company? The investigator? It's Kevin Johnson."

"Jesus, Mary, and Joseph, help us now," Bernadette threw up her hands. "You don't mean ... you can't mean that piece of work who was married to my granddaughter Darlene? The one who introduced you to what's his name who ran out on you?"

"One and the same," I admitted.

The ladies looked at each other and then at me.

"So, what are you going to do?" they asked in one voice.

"I don't know, that's the thing. Chester had a fit when I suggested I help him. He says I'll make things worse. He says he's an adult."

"That," Bernadette announced, "is nonsense. Your child is your child, no matter how old they are. You want to protect them. If they know you're doing it or not."

"But what does that look like?" I asked. "I can't talk to Darlene, Stuart, or any of my family. Who's going to help me?"

Joyce looked at me with surprise.

"Other mothers," she said. "Old ones. Us, we understand." She reached for her cane and stood up. "Ladies, to the dining room. This calls for tea."

CHAPTER TWELVE

I followed Joyce, Bernadette, and Minnie into the Manor's dining room. We sat down at their regular table near the window, with its view of the working wharf of Gasper's Cove. These women, all fishermen's widows, had spent most of their lives with one eye on the ocean, hoping all boats would come home each night.

They understood worry.

Joyce took charge. "This is the way I see it," she said. "If, and that's an *if*, some bad person set the cottage on fire, the best way to prove your boy wasn't involved is to find out who did it."

"Our fabric is in the middle of what this is about," Minnie interrupted. "That's for sure."

The table, excluding me, nodded in agreement.

"But I found remnants of the fabric in Halifax," I protested. "Who'd go into a secret hiding place, pull out bolts of fabric, donate it to a thrift store, and then go back and set a cottage on fire? That makes not one bit of sense."

"You might have a point there," Bernadette conceded. "But people do strange things all the time. And like you said yourself, the logical explanation from the insurance company's point of view might be that your out-of-work son did it. He didn't. He's a fine boy. Everyone knows that."

Joyce agreed. "Absolutely. Besides, I don't trust logic, but there's something I trust even less."

"What's that?" I asked.

"Coincidences." Joyce looked out the window to something only she could see on the horizon between the sky and the water. "There's no such thing. The fact that after all this time, as soon as we go looking for our fabric, the place where it was stashed away burned down is no accident. Just like all those other strange goings-on up and down the shore."

"What strange goings-on?" I asked.

Joyce looked at Bernadette and Minnie. "We've been hearing stories, haven't we, girls?"

"Like what? From who?" I asked.

"Our network," Minnie said. "Our connections."

"We hear everything," Bernadette explained. "Visitors, family, the staff here. This community is a chatty place. Weirdness is out there. We don't like that, so we're trying to figure it out."

Joyce saw I was confused. "Lots of small things, but when you have the big picture, like we do, it adds up. It started over the summer, around the time the renters came in. Things you wouldn't notice right away. Most in the vacation places the owners turn over to visitors and then don't go back into until the fall. Two cases of pepper shakers being stolen—not the salt, just the peppers. At two different addresses. That's what got our attention. I mean, who would want to break up a set like that?"

"And remember the cat bowls?" Minnie added. "Disappeared in at least three other places that we heard about. And a pillowcase right off the bed. Another place, a granny square afghan."

"Or the *Spring* gone from a set of four-season plates on the wall," Joyce added. "That one seemed sort of mean. A few things missing from garages too. The basket from a bicycle, box of Christmas lights."

"Speaking of lights," Bernadette added, "your fire wasn't the only one. Someone set fire to an old outhouse over on the edge of Drummond, if you can believe that. And a chicken coop, just last week."

This one shocked me. "Oh, no! The poor chickens!"

"Relax," Joyce said. "The chickens were fine. That retired professor from the city had already brought them into her house for the winter."

"Inside? Her house?" I asked. "How many?"

"More than I would want on my own dining room table, I can tell you that. Winter's long around here," Bernadette said. "But you know these people from the university. Not so much sense."

"True enough," Joyce said. "But that's my point. What happened to your family cottage, and to our fabric, is part of some kind of a larger operation. We just have to track it down."

"I'd have no idea where to start with that," I said.

"I've been working on it," Joyce said. "There are two possibilities I can think of."

"What are they?" I asked.

"Remember when I said that whoever took the fabric didn't know they had something valuable and were in there looking for something else?" she asked. I nodded. "We have to find out what that other thing could be." Joyce was thinking hard. "I would also be interested in how this person knew about the hidden place in the cottage. That would tell us a lot."

I couldn't disagree with that. "And you said you had another idea? What was that?"

"Based on my own experience, the most common explanation for random things disappearing is someone from behind the veil," Joyce said.

"You mean the other side of the causeway?" I asked. "Teenagers?" I remembered what Wade had said about vandalism when he'd come into the store.

"Please," Joyce gave me a look that showed she was disappointed in me. "Young people get blamed for everything. Most of the time, it's not them."

"Then, who?" I asked.

"Spirits." Joyce seemed to be more sure of this explanation the longer she considered it. "Think about it. A woman shows up and claims she can talk to the other side and tries to make money doing it. It never pays to cheapen a ghost. This lady moved around, from rental to rental. Maybe they followed her around and stirred things up."

"But ghosts wouldn't start a fire, would they?" I asked, playing along. It didn't seem to me that the other-worldly angle would get very far with Creepy Kevin.

"No, of course they wouldn't have started a fire," Joyce said. "That's not how the departed work. Something that destructive could only be done by a living human, with encouragement. The question is, who? We've got to move on this." Joyce leaned closer to me, both hands tight on her cane, the knuckles white. "That's where you and Darlene come in."

"Us?"

"We'll work on our end, but you deal with the RCMP. No point in duplicating resources. Talk to Wade Corkum and see if the Mounties have any interest in this," Joyce said. "Sneak in a few fire and things-gone-missing questions." She eyed me as if assessing my capabilities. "Slide it in. Talk about the weather."

"Got it," I said. "What is Darlene supposed to do?"

Joyce turned to Darlene's grandmother.

"We have to know how the insurance investigations are going," Bernadette said. "And Darlene used to be married to the guy doing the investigations. None of us can stand Kevin after what he did to her, or to you, but he does have one weakness."

"Darlene," I sighed.

"I'm afraid so," Bernadette said. "If anyone can get information out of Kevin, it would be her." She paused. "I hate to ask Darlene to do it, but talk to her. We have no choice. This is about family."

And that, in Gasper's Cove, was all that mattered.

CHAPTER THIRTEEN

Before I left Seaview Manor, the ladies made me promise I would talk to Darlene. I wasn't looking forward to that conversation.

Kevin knew something about me that Darlene did not. He knew about the letter I'd never delivered. The one I'd read, torn into tiny pieces, and stuffed into the bottom of a roadside trash can. If Kevin and Darlene talked, she might find out about it. And what would that do to our relationship?

I had to tell her everything myself, as soon as I could.

As it turned out, I was too late.

When I got to Darlene's house on Flying Cloud Drive, there was a car in her driveway. A car I'd last seen pulling away from Stuart Campbell's office. Kevin Johnson was inside the house. I circled the street and then drove past again slowly to make sure. When I did, a cat in the window made eye contact, a professional stalker dismissing the work of an amateur. Caught in the act, I picked up the pace and drove home to my dog.

I had left Toby alone in the house most of the day. He deserved a long walk. So, instead of following our usual route down to the elementary school, we went to the much bigger field beside Gasper's Cove Junior High. Often empty late on Saturdays, it was a perfect place to let Toby off leash to run full throttle. But today, we weren't the only ones there.

"Hey, Wade." I'd recognized the RCMP officer's shiny head when he came out of the exit door of the gym. "Back at school?"

"Nay," he laughed. "Getting the gear sorted out. I coach baseball in the summer, hockey in the winter. Good kids."

"I'm impressed," I said. "That's a lot of coaching. But not as glamorous as working with the Maple Leafs."

Wade snorted. "It's a lot better. The best thing I ever did was to see inside the NHL. Not the place for me."

This surprised me. As long as I had known Wade, he was the could-have-been-someone guy. The local star who had blown his shoulder the week before tryouts, and with it his chance of a gold-plated career with the National Hockey League. Wade's dream had been the dream of every boy who had ever laced up skates in Canada, his loss the sorrow of every young player who had never quite made it, the shadow forever attached to them, Peter Pans left to grow up on their own.

"Really? Why?"

"Simple." Wade had obviously thought about this a lot and now, in a junior high sports field, seemed ready to share it. "It was probably different in the old days, but the NHL isn't really about the hockey anymore. Now, it's about money, lawyers, and contracts. It's about Instagram girlfriends and buying a car for parents you don't have time to see anymore. Not my kind of hockey. The game I love is here."

"In Gasper's Cove?" I asked.

"Yeah. Hockey comes from backyard rinks and small communities. We invented the game." Wade looked at the horizon and into his past. "It's kept going by dads in cold Januarys with a hose. Guys who go out every night at 10 p.m. to check the ice and water it down. It's small trophies on the mantelpiece. It's old-timer's leagues. It's dryers down in the basement covered with dents from all the pucks that have been fired into the open door night after night. It's grandparents who don't miss any games and bring their own blankets. It's women with cowbells behind the bench and fathers standing with Tim Horton coffees in their hands. It's the guys who drive the Zambonis and who sharpen the skates." He paused and looked at me. "It's not about the accountants."

Chester had worked as an accountant.

Wade kept going. "I know you're upset CJ wants to join the RCMP. I saw your face when he told you. I didn't talk him into it," he said. "It was his idea."

In my heart, I knew Wade was right. "It seems so risky, dangerous, when he could have such a good life with the bank ...," I said, trailing off.

"Your idea of a good life," Wade corrected. "Not his. If he doesn't go for it now, it will hang over his head his whole life. What do they call it? The road not taken. That's not something you would want to wish on anyone. I should know. I wasted a lot of years doing that myself."

"You're right," I said, and he was. "But what do you think his chances are of getting in? He left his job."

"Good, I'd say," Wade said. "His employer wrote him a decent reference. He's got a strong academic background, the right reasons for joining." He stopped, and his eyes narrowed. "Something else is on your mind," he said. "What is it?"

"The insurance company is investigating the fire at the cottage …" I didn't want to say the rest of it.

"Ah, got it," Wade said. "We'll see how that plays out. We're looking at other angles right now." He bent down to pat Toby. "Anything you can tell us about Twyla Waters?"

That caught me off guard.

"Not much," I admitted. "She was supposed to be the last tenant at the cottage of the season. Chester, I mean CJ, would have told you that. He handled it all online. The only other thing I know is that she ran some kind of séances. Harry Sutherland and his mom went to see her." What else had Harry said? "Oh, yes, and Harry told me she had an argument with the new manager of the yacht club. But that comes from Harry, so who knows what really happened."

Wade put on his wrap-around sunglasses and considered this information.

"I'll check that out," he said. "Interesting. Could mean anything. They used to be married."

After Wade left and Toby and I finished our walk, I went home, made tea, and called Chester. Our last conversation had not been a good one. That bothered me.

"Yo, Mom. What's happening?" Chester answered. He sounded rushed and distracted.

"Not much," I lied. "How about yourself?"

"Been out surfing. Watched fireworks on the island last night. I'm going to work tomorrow at the Inn, helping Rollie cut back brush."

Briefly, I wondered if Chester found it easier to talk to Rollie than to me. After all, before Rollie had become an innkeeper, he had been a practicing psychologist. He'd know how to say the right things. I didn't always.

"Listen, I didn't mean to get pushy the other day," I said.

"All good," Chester said. "I think I was a bit tough on you myself. I just don't want my mom to worry, not at my age. Okay?" He hesitated. "Why don't you swing by the Inn tomorrow and we can hang out? Bring Toby." I heard a crunch of gravel, as if Chester was walking down a driveway away from a crowd. "And Mom, I need a favor, a big one. Got to show you. Can't do it over the phone."

My hand felt damp on my phone. I'd had enough surprises for one week.

"Sure," I said carefully. "See you before lunch?"

"Awesome. You can have a look, but you can say no. Love you, Mom. Later."

Chester hung up and was gone.

Toby came over and leaned against my legs.

I looked down at the only sensible member of my family. "Kids," I said to him. "Sometimes, I think I should have stuck to dogs."

From the look in his eyes, I believed Toby agreed with me.

CHAPTER FOURTEEN

When I arrived at the Inn the next day, Chester and Rollie were deep in the bushes at the edge of the lawn. They both wore safety glasses, heavy overalls, gloves, and headphones to muffle the racket of the chainsaws in their hands. Boys being boys, they were totally absorbed in cutting things up and throwing them around. They didn't seem to notice when I pulled in and parked.

I got out of the car and walked around so I was in front of them.

"Lot of work," I yelled. "What's going on?"

Rollie pulled his headphones down around his neck. His face was flushed above his beard, his red and gray cowlick stiff with sweat at his hairline.

"Visit from the fire department," he said. "After what happened at the cottage, they're making the rounds. It's been a dry summer. The fire hazard is higher than usual. They told us to cut the brush closest to our buildings, just to be safe."

That made sense. It also explained the huge pile of branches piled on the lawn.

"Great workout!" Chester beamed. "Nice to see you, Mom. Come to help?"

"Not with this," I said. "You asked me to come out, remember? Something urgent you wanted to show me?"

"Right on, gotcha." Chester pulled off his gloves and tossed his headphones into a toolbox on the ground. "It's inside. Let's go have a look. Give me a minute. I'll meet you in the dining room."

Once we were inside the Inn, Chester bounded up the stairs to the rooms on the second floor and left me to make my way to the Inn's burgundy and white Victorian dining room. In the hallway, I passed rows of photos, framed black and whites, of famous past residents of the island, a senator, a singer, and Billy something, once rumored to be the strongest man in the province. Opposite this gallery was a small alcove that Catherine, the town's former librarian, and now Rollie's partner in love and business, referred to as "the library." Catherine was in there now, up on a small footstool, pencil behind her ear, muttering.

"Hi," I said. "You look busy. How's the library?"

Catherine stepped down off the stool and faced me. She had a small card in her hand. "Incomplete." She held the catalog card closer so I could read it. The title and publication information had been typed with an old manual typewriter. Some of the letters were faint, some smudged red and black, the "Rs" all slightly raised, as if the typewriter ribbon had been dried out or one of the keys had stuck. The sight of it reminded me of my father, tapping away in the evening down in the basement.

I took the card from Catherine and read it.

```
Webster, Donald Blake, ed.

The Book of Canadian Antiques.

New York: McGraw-Hill

Book Company, 1974.
```

I handed the card back. "What's the problem?" I asked.

Catherine took the card and placed it in the open drawer of a small wooden cabinet, placing it upright, vertically, as if it wasn't ready to be refiled yet. She sat down on one of the brocade wing chairs and sighed.

"Why do I trust people?" she asked.

I had never found Catherine particularly reckless, or trusting, but I didn't bring that up. "Why, what happened?" I asked instead.

Catherine spread her arms out to encompass the whole of her library. "I built up this collection for our guests. Canadian and Atlantic fiction, guides to local flora, fauna, and sea life. Regional history, a few sea captain memoirs, and, of course, reference books"—she pointed to the card standing in the open drawer—"like this one. The books are meant to be read on the premises and returned when a guest leaves. Sometimes, if it is a novel that someone hasn't finished, they take it with them, which is why I keep the popular fiction in paperbacks. But loss doesn't happen often, and the reference books are usually read right here."

"Are you saying that this antiques book is missing?" I asked.

"Exactly, it's an older edition, virtually mint condition, and it's gone. I was sure, so sure, it was here on the shelves yesterday. But when I went to consult it, it was gone." Catherine shook her head in disbelief that her honor system had not been honored. "I've looked everywhere—checked the porch, the guests' rooms. Muriel Hirtle was here helping me clean, and neither of us could find it anywhere." Catherine tried to regain her composure and failed. "It was signed by the editor. It's irreplaceable."

I didn't know what to say. I was not a librarian.

"I'd love to help you look for it," I said, "but Chester has something he wants to show me. I'm on my way to the dining room to see what it is."

Catherine pulled herself out of her book grief long enough to refocus on me.

"Oh, that," she said. "It would be too much for me, but maybe you can do it. Good luck."

Confused and now worried, I looked down the hall. At the far end, a door opened, and my son poked his head out.

"Hey, Mom. Come on down. See what you think."

I shrugged at Catherine and hustled off.

When I arrived in the dining room, Chester was standing next to the big mahogany table. On it was a suit, pants and jacket, arranged as if they were laid out to contain the invisible man.

"What's this?" I asked, automatically reaching to feel the fabric. It was gray, silk and wool blend, with maybe, regrettably, a touch of polyester. The pants were slim, and the jacket had two buttons and two vent pockets. It was a modern but classic style, more fitted, and the pants tighter and shorter than I would have made them. The jacket had a stray thread hanging from one of the buttonholes. This was a new suit. But why was it here?

"You getting married?" I asked, looking around to see if there was a girl behind the fern in the room's big bay window. "Is that what this is about?"

"Mom." Chester put his hands on my shoulders. "Give it up. Not getting married. This is for my interview with the RCMP. I ordered it online, cost me a fortune, but it needs a little tweaking."

"Online?" I asked. "You didn't go to a tailor?"

"No one does anymore, not guys my age. I sent in my measurements, they generated a 3D model, I chose the fabric, it's something they call "mélange," and they turned it around in four days. Great concept, thinking of investing in the company. Did it all on my phone."

"But it doesn't fit?" I asked. That he could do it on the phone seemed important to Chester, the fit a mere detail.

Chester shrugged. "They have an alteration service and a satisfaction guarantee, but that means I have to return it and wait for it to come back. Seems like a hassle when I have the world's best sewer right here. You don't have to do it," he said with confidence that I would. "But I know how you like to sew. I was thinking if you could do something and leave it out on the step for me to pick up on my way to surfing?"

"Put it on. Let's see what we got." I pulled the measuring tape I kept in my purse out and got ready to work.

As it turned out, Chester's mail-order suit needed major adjustments. The waist of the pants needed to be let out and the princess seams in the back of the jacket taken in. This, of course, meant that I would have to open up the whole jacket and take in both the "mélange" fabric and the lining.

"No problem," I said. "Easy," I lied. My son's faith in my skills gave us a connection. I knew what I had to say. "This interview matters. I'll do a good job."

Chester hugged me, then went back outside. Alteration project in hand, I followed him out.

Rollie walked over to me.

"Thanks for giving Chester a place to stay and a job," I said to him.

"Not to worry," Rollie said. "He's a great guy." He pointed to the suit bag over my arm. "Ah, I see you're doing the sewing for the big interview. Glad to see you're coming around to the idea of your son the Mountie." I knew I'd be up most of the night to get this suit fixed, but it wouldn't be the first time I stayed up late to get a rush job done.

"Trying to," I said. "Don't have much choice, do I? Got a lot on my mind."

"Like what?" Rollie asked. I noticed he had made a subtle shift into his counselor's voice. "Talk to me."

"Where do I start? The cottage, the fire." I said. "And I guess you heard that Darlene's ex is back. He's working as some so-called insurance investigator for his dad. If it's arson, they won't pay out, you know."

"I do know that," Rollie said, "but don't get ahead of yourself."

"That's not everything," I continued. "It's strange, complicated. That woman who died, our renter? She was staying up and down the coast, I hear, at a bunch of places. And guess what? Weird stuff has been disappearing in a lot of those rentals."

"Tell me why where she stayed matters to you," Rollie said.

I hated it when he stopped sounding like my cousin and reverted to his professional voice. "It matters"—I had to be careful what I said—"because I think some of the things that were taken out of properties turned up in a thrift store in Halifax. How did that happen? Did it walk there from Gasper's Cove?"

"Relax," Rollie said. "Try to relax. Maybe you should consider that you are seeing connections where there aren't any. Maybe there's nothing to it."

My cousin's soothing voice, often reassuring, annoyed me now.

"Okay, then," I said. "Say odd things here and there are disappearing. And some of them are turning up in unusual places. If you were asked, in your *professional* opinion, what could make something like that happen, for argument's sake, what would you say?"

"Well," Rollie said after a long pause, "one first thing that comes to mind would be one of the impulse control disorders."

"What are they?" I asked.

"Actions that an individual has trouble resisting. Repetitive, often illogical behaviors that often occur in some sort of an attempt to self-soothe," he explained.

"Name some," I said. "Not sure what you mean."

"Compulsive shopping, cleaning, handwashing, some aspects of substance abuse, binge eating." He paused and looked at me. " Some of them have *mania* in the name, because of the compulsive aspect ..."

"Kleptomania," I interrupted. "Taking things because you can't control yourself." I'd heard once about a radio announcer who had a habit of taking the microphone home in his pocket.

Rollie nodded. "That's one of the disorders," he admitted, "but I'm not saying that is a possibility here. These conditions can be difficult to diagnose. They can come and go. Be gone for years then remerge suddenly when there's a major life change."

Something flickered in my memory, but I couldn't catch it. "Really? So, it might be a person who suddenly has a lot of stress in their life?"

"That could certainly be a trigger," Rollie said, then stopped himself. "Hey, Val, I was speaking academically. I know you. Don't try to use what I just said to try and figure anything out."

"Not a chance," I said. But we both knew that was a lie.

CHAPTER FIFTEEN

The wheels were turning on the ride home from the Bluenose Inn, and not only on the car. My mind was going too. Well over the speed limit. Why hadn't I thought of this before? Twyla Waters stayed up and down the coast in short-term rentals. The kind of places where things went missing.

"Who said a mystic can't be a kleptomaniac?" I asked the interior of the car. This would explain everything, or most of it, or some of it, or maybe only a little bit of it. But it was a start.

And then, because I was a genius, I had another flash of inspiration, an even better idea: Catherine's missing reference book on antiques valuation. Of course. Twyla stayed in old places not to look for ghosts or let her impulses run free but to find vintage treasures. And anything she took that turned out not to be of value, she dumped in a Frenchy's donation box.

It all fit so neatly, like a well-drafted facing on a sheath dress.

But wait. I slowed down to the speed limit. How would I prove it? Twyla was gone. What did I know about her?

Not much.

Who did?

Someone who had once married her, and fought with her, in public. What about? Harry had told me. Oh, yes.

The past.

I saw the sign ahead. I made an abrupt turn.

The Gasper's Cove Yacht Club was once a simple operation. For years, it had been not much more than a boathouse and a dock with fuel, potable water, and a dinghy used to run sailors out to the boats tied up to bobbing buoys. The club then had suited local fishermen and weekend sailors, but an influx of fancier boats making short ports of call on their way down the coast had prompted the club to expand and live up to the yachting part of its name.

As a result, a new clubhouse had been built. Later, a deck was added to the back on the waterside, with a long counter and tall stools for the contemplation of the waves on sunny days. Since Peter arrived, the menu on the deck included arugula salad with basil tofu dressing, something few ordered, unlike the fish and chips with a side of coleslaw, which everyone did.

The parking lot was still gravel. When he saw me pull into it, Harry Sutherland ambled over to meet me.

"Know anything about raccoons?" he called out. "Good money if you do."

"No," I said, walking over to meet him. "We had some at the store, but Tommy Hirtle took care of them."

"Right," Harry said. "The old classical music trick. I tried that. Maybe I didn't have the right channel."

"Why don't you ask Tommy?" I looked around. "I thought he worked here, helping out."

Harry stepped closer to me. "Tommy's not around no more. Raccoons are safe," he confided. "Criminal background check got him."

"What are you talking about?" I asked.

"Peter the boss said it was standard practice in the industry. Anyone in a position of responsibility or public contact needed a background check to work here." Harry pulled his belt up. "I passed mine. Flying colors."

I admitted that this surprised me.

Harry appeared to feel the same way. "Never charged," he said. "Few misunderstandings, here and there. That's it. Not everyone sees the big picture right away."

I rolled my eyes at the ground. "But what does this have to do with Tommy?" I asked. "And raccoons?"

"That's the thing, isn't it? You'd think nothing. Mr. Rules here said that anyone getting a dime out of the club, raccoon hunting included, needed to have their past checked out." Harry snorted. "Old Tommy heard that, and he downed tools and took off, even moved his boat out. You never know, do you, about people?"

I couldn't argue with that. "Peter around?"

"He's in the boathouse. Why do you want to see him?" Harry asked.

I scrambled for a reason that would make sense to Harry.

"To offer my sympathies. Twyla, the woman who died in the fire, was his ex-wife," I explained. "I heard that from a reliable source."

"Get out of town," Harry whistled. "Talk about the odd couple. Explains the latest fight a few days ago."

"Another fight?" I asked. "What was that one about?" I wondered if these disagreements were as public as Harry said or if Harry was one to listen in.

Harry shrugged. "The usual," he said. "What sets most wife-type women off? She yelled at him that he'd never change. As if that was a thing. Which it isn't."

I had no idea what Harry was talking about. "What do you mean?"

"Men don't change," Harry said, as if this was a rule of the universe. "Don't know how to. Don't want to. What you see is what you get." A weak revelation drifted across his face. "You don't think that's why, do you?" he asked.

"Why what?"

"The reason I'm still single? When I got so much going for me?"

"I'm sure that's not why," I said as an evasion. "You just haven't met the right person."

Harry's face relaxed back into his default, self-satisfaction. "True enough," he said. "Got pretty high standards. Otherwise..." He looked me over, then caught himself. "Not to worry, Val, lots of other men out there looking for a sturdy woman. Someone for everyone."

I studied the dandelions in the grass. Not all of Gasper's Cove's pests grew in the ground.

"Peter is in the boathouse?" I asked again. It was an exit line, not a statement, not a question. "I don't want to miss him."

"Right on," Harry said, patting my arm. "You hang in there, dear."

The inside of the boathouse was cool, dark, and, after Harry, reasonable and well-ordered. Built at the far end of the dock, it stored everything a boater might need. Marine paint, tools, engine parts, tins of oil, and big red gas cans with long yellow spouts like the beaks of a bird. It had coils of rope hanging from the ceiling, flags from past regattas on the walls, and rows and rows of life jackets lined up near the door. The building itself was long, at least 50 feet. The wall away from the water was filled with deep racks. These held masts, oars, sails wrapped tight like cigars, small two-person open boats, with only narrow bench seats, thin Lasers for racing, canoes, paddleboards, and kayaks. Two large sliding doors, wooden with X-bracing, hung from barn-door hardware. One was closed, the other open, both leading with narrow ramps down to the dock outside. The boards of the floor were wide and rough, with rollers set in it three feet apart for sliding the boats toward the outside and the waves.

At first, I didn't see the manager, but I could hear him. I followed the sound of sanding wood. Off in a corner, Peter Tupper was bent over a large wooden cabinet he appeared to be refinishing. I knocked into an oar leaning against a rack. Startled by the noise, Peter turned to see me.

"Can I help you?" he said, making clear he had identified me as a non-sailor and, as such, someone who had no business being in his boathouse. "Members only," he added, in case I had missed the point. He caught me looking at an almost-but-not-quite familiar object on his workbench.

"That's a drone," he said, gently rearranging it next to the control unit, the drone's fins spread out, so it resembled a miniature alien spaceship. "Someone left it here. Harry, maybe. He used it in hurricane season, I think, to check on damage to the boats and the coast. Erosion that might impact safe passage through the channel." He smiled to himself. "Myself, I would have used it to look for illegal fishing, unregistered lobster traps."

"I can see Harry playing with toys," I said.

Peter snorted and crossed his arms over a large, oiled canvas work apron. "You didn't tell me why you're here," he said and waited. The air outside had been cool and breezy. Inside the boathouse, it felt warmer, damp, and close. It had the moldy smell of bilge water and seaweed that had been tangled in ropes and was now quietly decaying, a scent cut through by the defiant tang of the sea, the irresistible salty smell of adventure that had pulled sailors away from the safety of the land to the uncertainty of the water for thousands of years. Mixed in with these dockside smells, of salt, old fish, and oil, I picked up something stronger. I noticed a stack of old towels and an open can of tung oil on the workbench beside the cabinet. When the sanding was finished, Peter would rub the oil into the wood. And then, to emphasize that I was holding up the restoration operations, Peter picked up the can and screwed on a red plastic cap, turning it so I saw the label *Circa 1850*, a flame, and *Caution Attention: Read instructions before using. Lire les instructions avant usage.* A traditional product for a traditional job.

"That will look beautiful oiled," I said. "What is it?" The cabinet was chest high and deep, with a dozen or more drawers, each less than five inches high, all shallow and faced with brass scrolled handles under the frames of small, perfect card holders.

"A map cabinet, obviously," Peter snapped, his thin little mustache a straight line above his mouth. "One of our members, Stuart Campbell, bought it at a government surplus auction but couldn't get it up the stairs to his office." Peter wiped his hands on one of the towels and smiled. Stuart's loss had been his gain. "So, he gave it to the club, for nautical maps. When I'm done with it, I'm going to put it in the clubhouse. Now, again, why are you here? I'm sure it's not to discuss antique furniture."

"I just found out that the poor woman who died in the fire was your former wife." This was an awkward start to any conversation, but the best I could do. "I wanted to offer my sympathies."

"Well, you've done that," Peter said. "Anything else?"

I searched for something else to say. "If there's anything you need," I offered. "A casserole? Someone to talk to? I know you're new here." In Gasper's Cove, whenever anyone lost someone, it was customary to visit on a rotating schedule and to flood the house with sweet-and-sour meatballs, for-the-freezer pans of lasagna, and Nanaimo bars. If there was another way to mourn, I didn't know it. "I'm so sorry. I didn't get a chance to know her very well. Would you like to talk about her?" I asked. About her criminal background, I wanted to add, or why she didn't refinish antiques but stole them.

Peter stared up at the rafters of masts and rope before answering me. "I don't need casseroles, and I don't need sympathy. It was a lousy way to go, but Twyla and I were married years ago. It was an office romance thing that should never have gone further. We lost touch. And that was fine with both of us." This felt like a speech Peter had repeated many times before, if only to himself. "To tell you the truth, no one was more surprised than I was when she turned up in town."

This was interesting information. I was glad I'd come. "Why is that?" I asked.

"At first, I thought she had followed me here." Peter laughed at his vanity. "But that didn't make sense after all this time. And all that moving around, rental to rental, claiming she was trying to commune with the spirits? Where did that come from? Twyla was about as spiritual as a bar of soap. Maybe it was a change-of-life thing. You couldn't trust her. Turn your back, and she'd sell you out in a minute if she could." He snorted. "She had some sort of angle that brought her up here. Had to. I tried to get it out of her. That didn't go well. She laughed at this job, at me. Said I couldn't see the big picture if I fell over it." He glared at me, as if all we change-of-life women were responsible for each other. "Now she's gone, maybe there is someone somewhere who'll miss her, but it won't be me."

I hesitated. "So, no casserole?" I asked, to make sure.

"What do you think?" Peter turned his back on me, picked up his can of finishing oil, and unscrewed the top.

There was nothing else to say.

But I had what I came for.

CHAPTER SIXTEEN

As soon as I was back in the car, I reached for my phone. Once, in a moment of weakness, Wade had given me his cell number. I dialed it now.

It went to voicemail.

I left a message.

Wade? Valerie Rankin. Remember you asked me to tell you if I noticed anything strange? I've been on it, and I am pretty sure Twyla Waters, that woman who died in the fire at the cottage, which sure was the wrong place at the wrong time, was the thief who was taking things up and down the coast, not teenage vandals, which, speaking as a mother, makes me feel better. Back to Twyla. She was trying to steal antiques. I'm going to leave the evidence part up to you. But I am pretty sure I am right.

I paused and tried to think of how to make my suspicions sound more official. I added

Over and out.

I went to put my phone away, satisfied I had helped the Mounties get their man, when I saw I had a voicemail of my own.

Hey, Mom. This is CJ. Sorry I missed you, but I'm going down to Halifax. Got the call about my RCMP interview. Wade's taking me in. Wish me luck.

For the first time since Chester had said he wanted to join up, I could see a positive side to it. Now, it would be like we were working together.

I still hadn't heard from Wade by the next morning, but I was sure I would soon. The bag with Chester's suit in it was no longer on the front step. It was a clear late summer day, and I felt a new season, a sense of completion, and peace. By the time Toby and I arrived at the store, Colleen had already opened.

I was ready to get to work.

"You didn't need to rush in," Colleen said. "Muriel was waiting at the door when I got here. She's already up in the Co-op, tidying up. She said she wanted to talk to you."

"Do you know what about?"

Colleen shrugged. "Not sure, but it seemed to me it was why she was here so early. She wanted to see you before we got busy."

She was right. These days, we were busy, and glad for it. For a while, it had seemed that Rankin's, like many family-owned stores in rural Nova Scotia, was doomed to be swept away by the Walmarts and progress. But then we noticed how people from away valued our traditional handcrafts. That led me to set up a retail space in the store's underused upstairs. We called it the Gasper's Cove Crafters: A Community Co-op, a place where anyone in the community who made things (which described most of us) could sell on consignment. We now represented sewers, quilters, knitters, painters, potters, carvers, plant macrame holder makers, tea towel embroiderers (the list was as long as the Nova Scotia winters) from all across the island. The crafters themselves ran the Co-op, as volunteers, on a rotating basis. This was one of Muriel Hirtle's days.

She put down her roll of pricing stickers as soon as I reached the top of the stairs.

"Good morning, Valerie," she said. "Just catching up. Do you have time for a word?"

"Of course," I said. Under her new perm, Muriel's face was as tight as her curls.

She took a big breath. "It's about Tommy. I'm worried." Muriel fixed her gaze on a stack of tea towels a local artist had stenciled with line drawings of Nova Scotia lighthouses. "About his little problem. I hope you don't think the worst of him. It's come and gone over the years. Me and his brother handled it. If something was missing, we'd talk to the people or put things back before anyone knew they were gone. Sometimes, we'd just get rid of it, smoothed it over for him. Except that one time in the city when the police caught him."

I didn't say anything. My mind was too busy processing what I was hearing.

"Tom hasn't been having an easy time of it since he retired. His brother's not here to help me anymore. Being out on the water was always the best thing for him, calmed him down. But now, he's back on land all the time ... when he gets restless, it gets worse." The faded blue eyes behind Muriel's bifocals were large and pleading. "Sometimes, he doesn't even know he's doing it. It's like ... what it's like? ... sleepwalking. As if he's in some kind of a trance. Like some people walk around the house at night, in their pajamas, go into the kitchen, and pour themselves a glass of milk. And the next morning, they don't know why there's that glass on the counter. Except with Tommy, it's in the daytime, and it's not milk."

It matched, better than a facing. The stories from property owners had begun only this season around when Muriel had started cleaning. And I remembered she had said Tommy had come with her when she worked.

"But didn't you notice"—I tried to find a way to say this that wouldn't hurt Muriel's feelings—"that he was taking things while you cleaned?"

Muriel put the roll of stickers down on the counter. "I kept an eye on him. But he wasn't doing it when I was there. I started to notice bags in the back of the car when he went to Halifax for his dental work. I realized he was taking things I didn't recognize and getting rid of them outside the community. That got me worried. So, I went searching. I found the list in the garage. He'd been into my phone and looked up the codes to open the doors to my jobs. But I fixed that."

"How?"

"The password to my phone was my birthday, but I changed it," she laughed, "to something no man would ever think of."

"What's that?" I asked.

"The date of our anniversary. After I did that, nothing's gone missing at any of my places. I fixed it," Muriel said. "I wanted to talk to you because I was thinking of sending him over to talk to Rollie. He's your cousin. He used to be a sort of doctor. Maybe you could let him know what's going on?"

I reached over and hugged Muriel. She was smaller and thinner than I'd thought.

"I'll talk to Rollie," I promised. "He'll know what to do, don't you worry."

Muriel's narrow shoulders dropped with relief.

"Not that he's so bad now, doesn't have the chance," she said. "He goes out to houses, but only to check out the raccoons. And there is always somebody watching what he does. People like to learn more about raccoons, you know. He even did a job for that cranky manager at the club, Peter Tupper. Peter said a person he knew was staying in a place that had raccoons. Tommy was able to use the code to get in, we'd cleaned there before. Guess they went through it from one end to the other but couldn't find where any animal could get in. Turns out that doesn't matter anymore."

"Why's that?" I asked.

"Place burnt down the next day," Muriel said. "It was your cottage they were at."

When I got to the bottom of the stairs, I ducked behind a mop display on the main floor of the store and called Wade's number. This was one call I would have liked to have left as a message.

Wade picked up.

"Hey, Valerie. Call to wish your son good luck?" he asked. "I've just dropped him off for the interview. There was a lot of construction on the way, but we made it here in time."

"Already wished him luck. That's not why I called." I said. There was no way around this one but the truth. "I left you a message. Did you listen to it?"

"I didn't see the call from you until we were on the road," Wade said. I thought I detected a sigh. "Didn't check it yet— like I said, we got held up with the road building. A one-hour trip took two. We were running late.

"Great. Do me a favor will you?" I asked. "I made a mistake. Don't listen to it? Erase it. Forget you ever heard from me."

There was a moment of silence at the other end of the line.

"I think we've been here before, haven't we?" Wade asked. "Let me guess. You had one of your all-over-the-place theories and decided to alert the RCMP. Then, you thought about it. Am I right?"

"Maybe."

"Don't worry," Wade said. "Erased. Done."

"And one more thing." I wasn't sure how to say this. "Appreciate it if ..."

Wade finished my sentence for me. "... I didn't let CJ know about any of this?" I thought I heard sympathy in his voice. "Don't worry about it. We all make mistakes."

He wasn't wrong.

CHAPTER SEVENTEEN

I was hiding in a back booth at the Agapi, having lunch, when George came over.

He pointed to my cup with his coffee pot. "Refill?" he asked.

I nodded.

George looked around the restaurant. The lunch rush was over. George wiped down the table, returned the pot to the hot pad at the side of the room, came back, and sat down.

At first, he didn't say anything. When he did, it was one word.

"Darlene."

"What's going on?" I asked. "I haven't talked to her much since we made that trip to Halifax."

George sighed. "That's two of us, and that's my problem. I thought once we had the church thing all squared away, we were good to go." He glanced at Sophia across the room. "Since the priest gave us the okay, my mother has been on the phone to everyone. All the relatives. In Greece, Montreal, and Toronto. This one is going to be a real wedding, she's telling them." He paused. "It sounds more dramatic in Greek. Anyway, they're talking showers, dresses, who should be invited. Food, of course. I've even got an aunt in Mississauga working on the seating plan for our side."

"Sounds good," I said, "so what's the problem?"

"The bride. Geez, we waited long enough to get here, but something's telling me Darlene is getting cold feet." George started to reorder the little paper packets of sugar in their bowl as if it were the most important job in the world, avoiding my eyes.

"That is not true," I said. "I'm the one who went to Halifax to see the priest with her, remember? She was so wound up on the way there that she ate three bags of chips before we'd hit the city limits. I'd never seen her as happy as she was when she came out of that church."

"If that's true," George asked, "then why won't she set the date? You try explaining that one to my mother. Or my future mother-in-law. Something's changed. I don't want to even consider it, but I think I know what, or who, it is. It's that guy, Kevin. She said something about needing closure. Closure? Darlene doesn't talk like that. And I don't trust that guy."

Nobody did. I was at the top of that list. But I knew that part of this problem was something I'd done. George deserved to know.

"Look, there's something I have to tell you," I said. "Kevin was, is, and always will be bad news and a jerk. The problem for Darlene is, she's a good person, so she always has trouble understanding that someone else isn't. He ran around on her, just like his best bud, my ex-husband, ran around on me. In a strange way, when Darlene found out that Kevin had been covering up for my ex, it was the last straw for her, and she filed for divorce. Kevin didn't think she'd go through with it. He came into the store, tried to act sorry, and gave me a letter for me to give her because she wouldn't see him."

"I knew part of this, but not all of it," George said. "So, what happened?"

"Being me, I read the letter," I confessed. "It said all the usual stuff he always said, but he said that this time, he'd changed and wanted her back. He wanted to start a family, which is the one thing she'd wanted and he never did."

"Oh, hell," George said. "She would have been a great mother, never had the chance. What did she do when she read that?"

"She never saw it. I didn't give it to her. I didn't believe anything he said for a minute, and I didn't want her hurt." I looked out of the window as if surveying all my mistakes. "But that wasn't up to me. She needed to follow that relationship right to the end. I took that away from her. And that's what's happening to you. I'm sorry." I'd seen Kevin's car outside Darlene's house. By now, I was sure she knew what had happened. No wonder I hadn't heard from her.

George put his hand on top of mine. "Look, I would have done the same thing if I was you. Don't beat yourself up. It's going to be hard, but I'll give her space and let her figure it out. But I can tell you, I'm not going to sit here and do nothing."

"What do you mean?" I asked.

"This Kevin guy. We gotta get him out of here ASAP." There was anger in George's black eyes, and I was glad it wasn't directed at me. Darlene, if she came to her senses, should know how lucky she was. "You know him better than I do. What's it going to take to do that?"

Having shared my oldest and worst secret with him, I decided to tell George everything. I swore him to secrecy and told him about the ladies at Seaview and their crime. About how Kevin was here to investigate possible arson at the kids' cottage, and if he could prove it, according to Stuart, there would be no insurance money to rebuild.

To give George credit, he listened quietly, without judgment or interruption, before he said anything.

"Hmm. Kevin is an insurance investigator. The sooner that wraps up, the sooner he goes, and everyone can go back to their lives. Am I right?"

"Pretty much describes it," I said. "But what can we do to make that happen? Nothing."

"Not so sure about that," George said. "I've got a suspicious streak. One thing that's bothered me about this fire is that maybe that's not the point. Maybe Twyla didn't die because she got caught there when it burned down in some insurance scam like this guy Kevin might think, but that the fire was set to get rid of her—if not kill her, at least scare her off."

"But who here would want to kill her?" I asked. "She came from away. I had a theory about her, but it was a dumb one. From what I know, all she did was pretend to chase ghosts and charge people for her services as a mystic. Pretty harmless."

George looked at me, calculating the situation and its possibilities. "She wasn't the only person who came here from somewhere else. I heard she and Peter used to be married, but she dumped him, thought she could do better. No love lost there, from what I heard."

"Sounds about right," I said.

"I don't buy it that it was some kind of weird coincidence that they both ended up here in this small community they had never been to before, at the same time," George said. "Think about it. What are the chances? I'm sure one of them had something going, and the other one was following up on it." He paused to consider the possibilities. "Maybe she was blackmailing Peter. Or he had a scheme, and she wanted in on it. Or hate. From what I hear, Peter's a pretty uptight, play-by-the-rules kind of guy. Maybe he snapped at the sight of her, waited all these years to get back at her, or he found out she was breaking some kind of rule."

"Wow," I said, ashamed of the admiration in my voice. "That's a lot of motives for murder. How did you think of all of this?"

"You don't know anything about Greek history, do you?" George said. "We've been up to something for thousands of years. We think big."

"I can see that," I said. "But where does this leave us? If we could, and we can't prove the cottage was set on fire as a way to get rid of Twyla, and Peter did it, then Kevin would have no reason to be here."

George cut me off. "Darlene would set a date, and my mother and her mother could start sending out invitations."

"Sounds like we both want the same thing," I said. "But you've laid out a lot of options. Where do we start?"

"Well, we don't know what went on between them, no one on the outside ever does," George said. I wondered if he was talking about Peter and Twyla or about himself and

Darlene. "One thing that strikes me is that this woman moved around a lot. If you don't buy the ghostbuster theory, then it seems to me that she was looking for something. The question is, what?"

"I thought vintage knick-knacks, but that idea was a bust. What else is there?"

"No idea," George said, "but all this ghost talk makes me think there is something in Gasper's Cove's past that might be worth searching for. We need to talk to someone who knows the history of the area. A historian or something."

"I can do better than that," I said. "I know a group of local experts."

"Who?"

"The semi-criminal institutional memory of this whole community," I said. "And I know just where to find them."

"You do?"

"Sure do." I looked across the room at Sophia. "Can you ask your mother to pack up a dozen of her baklavas to go? I've got a tea party to go to."

CHAPTER EIGHTEEN

The cheerful middle-age woman behind the front desk at Seaview Manor put Max Factor down onto the floor. She greeted me with enthusiasm.

"They'll be glad to see you," she said. "The mayor's got them cornered in the multipurpose room. Meet and greet. He calls it 'voter contact,' keeping it warm until the next election. We had a hard time rounding up a crowd. But we caught them. A couple of the walkers got tangled, slowed the escape."

I'd been to Mayor Elliot Carter's presentations before. To say he was a dull speaker was an insult to dull speakers.

"When are they going to be done?" I asked. I had timed my visit to coincide with Joyce's tea party.

The receptionist looked up at the clock on the dusty rose wallpaper. "They should have been done twenty minutes ago. I need an excuse to break it up. Give me a minute."

I sat down on one of the visitor's chairs, the doorway to the multipurpose and dining rooms in my sights. I watched the receptionist bustle over to the room where Mayor Elliot

Clark was presumably holding forth, knock on the door, and go in.

Within minutes, the door was flung open, and a gaggle of the Manor's residents came out as fast as they could travel. Leading the exodus was Joyce, who smiled when she saw me, and even more when she noticed the Agapi pastry box in my lap.

"Valerie," she called out. "We were wondering what happened to you. Do you have time for tea?"

I lifted my box. "Why do you think I'm here? I've got treats."

"You go ahead," Joyce said, motioning to the dining room. "I'll tell the kitchen to put the kettle on and gather up the girls. There's something we should tell you."

Alone in the dining room, at the sunny table next to the window and the view of the water, I tried to assemble my thoughts. The situation felt the same as that stage of garment sewing after the cutting, when all the pieces seemed both strange and familiar, and the next step was to put the correct edges together. Was there something I was missing? Had I cut out the yoke for View A when what I really needed was View B? I had many of the pieces, but no idea what I was making. Maybe here at Seaview Manor, the ladies would help me find the instructions, assuming they could tell me everything I needed to know.

When Joyce, Minnie, and Bernadette arrived and arranged themselves around the table, I laid out Sophia's baklava on a plate and waited. "How was the mayor's talk?" I asked.

"The usual," Minnie sniffed. "Seniors always vote, so we have to put up with these politicians. But today, Mayor Carter seemed off his game."

"I noticed that too," Minnie said. "Heard he's no longer the commodore at the yacht club, that may be it, or the money he has to give back."

"What money?" I asked.

"Taxes," Bernadette explained. "Since Darlene's the deputy mayor, she knows all about it. She explained it to me. Years ago, the yacht club used to give free sailing lessons. Someone, back in the time when you would have been young Valerie, applied to have it made into a designated charity."

"And what does that mean?" I asked.

"What it means is that the town shouldn't have been collecting property taxes from the club. But they did, for years. Let me tell you, that adds up. So now, Peter Tupper is suing the council for back taxes. And that's going to blow Mr. Balance-the-Budget Elliot Carter's next election platform right out of the water. From what we saw today, I'd say it's taken the good right out of him."

I could only imagine.

In the last year, the mayor had spent considerable sums of money on his pet projects. Portable light-up signs on rural roads no one traveled, telling motorists they were going too fast. A twin city partnership with an equally obscure town in the Netherlands that involved us sending them salt cod and them shipping us spring tulips that lasted twenty-five minutes in the salt air off the Nova Scotia coast. There'd even been the brand-new Mayor's Grand Procession on Victoria Day weekend, featuring Elliot sitting in the back of a rented 1952 convertible covered in tissue roses made by his tired assistant. And as much as I loved a good DIY project, even I could see the car and parade had not been a good use of taxpayers' funds.

"But how did the club only find out about this now?" I asked. "After all these years?"

"Peter won't say, and it doesn't really matter. But I'm not sure how Mayor Elliot can get over this one. People only tolerated him because they thought he knew what he was doing. So much for that. What's he going to do now? It's not like our mayor has much of a personality to fall back on."

Any good gossip session, as a matter of protocol, required some reciprocation. "You know," I said, "the mayor and Peter knew each other when they both worked for the province. It's got to hurt to be caught out like that by an old colleague."

"That's interesting," Joyce said. "Maybe Peter had a score to settle. Who knows?"

She stopped and looked at a seagull outside on the window's ledge. It seemed to remind her of something. "Funny how Peter didn't want to talk about how he had family here when he was visiting," she said. "Who does that? It's obvious who his people are."

"The Tuppers," Bernadette cut in, "were all good-looking people, even with the ears."

"Real big ears," Minnie agreed. "That manager has the same kind of body they all had, short legs, what did they call it?"

"Built like a brick outhouse," Joyce volunteered. "That's what my dad used to call it. Peter has to be related, but our Tuppers moved away from here, geez, after the war."

"You're right, aren't you?" Minnie said. "The old fellow who built the cottage was a rumrunner like a lot of the men were. I'll have to check, but there may be a connection on my mother's side. Anyway, the son of the old guy tried to run for office, even with those ears. Lots of people have them. Look at one of my own grandsons. Cute as a bug's ear, pardon the expression, but he's got a pair on him, I swear a good wind'd catch them, and that boy would fly."

"I hope you didn't say that to his mother," Joyce said. "Now, back to business. But you first, Valerie. What do you have to tell us?"

I didn't know where to start. "Your fabric. I think I know what happened to it. I don't think there's any way you're ever going to get it back," I hurried on before the ladies could ask any questions. "Just a bit of mischief-making, I can't tell you who."

Joyce and Bernadette exchanged a look. "This person who took our fabric, and you don't want to talk about, did they say anything about what they did with the other stuff?"

"What other stuff?" I felt myself tense. "What else didn't you tell me?"

"No need to, we thought since fabric was your line of business, there was no point in going into the rest of it. One step at a time. But since we're not making any money on that stash, we need to tell you about the other assets," Minnie said. "Just in case some of it was still around, and we could sell that. We've got Christmas to think about."

"What else did you take?" I asked, trying to sound more rational than I felt.

"You mean then or after?" Minnie asked.

"I didn't know there was an after."

"There was, and there wasn't," Joyce added.

Bernadette leaned across the table toward me. "You see, when we went to put the fabric into the hiding place, the space wasn't quite empty ..."

"There might have been a bottle or two that we donated to our sewing circle, for special occasions," Minnie said.

"Like what kind of special occasions?" Did I know these women at all?

"Engagements, Easter, Christmas, finishing a nice hat, the day the snow melted ..."

"When we saw the first robin, tying off the last quilt ... We'd go back and dip into it."

"Stop it," I interrupted. I had had enough. "You're telling me you took some booze from a rumrunner's cupboard? What else did you take?"

"Take? Nothing!" Joyce was unreasonably indignant. "Just some old papers. But quite a few bottles in there, if you want to know the truth. We're wondering if you can find out if some of that's still around. Strong stuff like that doesn't go bad. After all this time, it might be better, worth more." Joyce was thoughtful. "If anyone had found it, or had drank any of it, you'd know."

"That's for sure," Minnie giggled. "No surprise it was hidden. What we took, we had to cut with juice."

"I remember, that stuff could take the paint off a car," Bernadette mused. "Hundred percent proof, if it was anything. That stuff was explosive."

I almost choked on my tea.

Half of Gasper's Cove, not to mention one insurance investigator, wanted to know why our cottage burned down and one woman was dead.

Was this the answer?

CHAPTER NINETEEN

Before I had even left the Manor's parking lot, I called George.

"Agapi Restaurant," he said. "Best Greek food this side of the causeway." The Agapi was the best, and only, restaurant in Gasper's Cove. "How can I be of service?"

"You can't," I said, whispering, although I was alone in the car. The confidentiality of my information seemed to require it. "Not food-wise. I have news. About what might have started the fire. But we've got to be careful how we get it out there—reputations are at stake."

George sounded interested and annoyed all at the same time. Handling those two emotions couldn't have been easy. "Forget that," he said. "We'll deal with reputations later. Tell me. What did you find out?"

"Booze," I said. "Old stuff, moonshine, maximum proof. Listen, I had a great-uncle, had a still downstairs in his house. Power went out, and he went down with a candle. Boom. Blew up the whole basement."

"What?" George asked. "Geez, what happened to your uncle?"

"Stopped drinking," I said, "but that's not the point. Twyla said she was a medium."

There was a pause. "Are you talking about those communing with the spirits things she ran? I don't see what that has to do with anything." I heard the deflation in George's voice. For a minute, he'd thought I had useful information to share.

"Ghosts, séances, think about it," I said. "Harry and his mom had a session with her, it was at night. You don't contact the spiritual world at ten o'clock on a Tuesday *morning*, do you? No. Particularly if you're faking it, going for effect." I saw the whole scene in my mind. A paisley shawl draped over Twyla's shoulders. Bangles halfway up to her elbows, an incense burner smoldering on a sideboard. Music playing from a hidden speaker, something instrumental, flutes maybe, tinkling, like fairy feet or broken ice on the snow. The drapes drawn, the room dusky. "Candles," I said. "If a mystic didn't use them, who would? We sell a ton at the Co-op, one of our best sellers. Not that I ever buy them, that's for sure."

"Why not?"

"Heard enough bad stories when I was a kid about kerosene lamps, candles, houses in the country burning down." I shuddered at the memories. "They're a fire hazard. I'd worry I'd fall asleep before I put them out."

"And with the moonshine you're talking about"—George was putting it together—"like flame to gasoline."

"You know what this means, don't you?"

"Yeah, I think I do," George whispered.

"This is the information that Creepy Kevin needs to hear. Much as I don't want to, I've got to get in touch with him."

"All right," George said. "Better do it and do it quick. Guy gives you any trouble, you know where to find me."

I did.

The trouble was, I didn't know where to find Darlene's ex-husband, once her financial dependent, now his father's. It was that office I called first.

"Johnson Insurance. How can I help you?" The voice on the phone sounded as if it belonged to a breathless twenty-year-old. Briefly, I wondered if old man Johnson was populating his business with any relative who needed a job. "Home, auto, business?" The late adolescent prompted, her voice distracted, as if in the background she was on her phone, checking her social media and listing the lines of business on automatic, as if they had no real meaning for her, which I was sure they did not. "Tenant? Motorcycle? High risk?"

"Nope," I said. "Got that covered. I just need a number for one of your agents, or investigator, whatever, Kevin Johnson. He's here in Gasper's Cove. I want to reach him."

"Kev? What's he doing up there?" There was a change in the girl's voice, as if Kevin's name had penetrated the high walls of her digital reality. "I thought he was on vacation. Florida? Or Portugal? I always forget which one."

This was interesting. The news that Kevin appeared to be up to something was oddly satisfying and validating. I didn't like change. And it looked like Creepy Kevin hadn't.

"I saw him here just the other day, and I was sure he said he was an insurance investigator, looking into a fire in the district. Did I get that wrong?" I asked.

"Kevin? An investigator? Of what? Maybe my uncle was trying to find him something new to do." I had been right about the family as employees. "Sales wasn't a good fit."

I really wanted to talk to Kevin now. "His number?" I reminded her. "A cell phone?"

The receptionist obliged and then tried to prolong our conversation. "Are you sure he's not on vacation?" she asked. "Real sure? He promised to bring me back something from the duty-free."

"Very sure," I said, wondering if I should tell this girl that I hoped a gift from an airport was all Kevin had promised her. "Thanks for the number. You take care of yourself."

Fortified by the fact I knew Kevin was lying about things big and small, I dialed his number. For once he, not me, had some explaining to do.

"Kevin here," he answered. I noted that unlike the receptionist at the head office, he didn't identify his company or role in his greeting. Maybe that's because he didn't have one, a position, that is. I could almost hear him reading my name on his phone display, moving his lips. "The lovely Val. I had a feeling I would hear from you," he purred in his patented bedroom voice. "What can I do you for?"

This is why Alexander Graham Bell invented the telephone: to keep men who talked like that out of smackdown reach. But I had to keep going, for my family's sake.

"Business call, Kev," I answered. Kevin used to hate it when anyone called him by the short form of his name. I hoped that was still true. "I have something you need to know about that fire at our cottage. Maybe we should talk about it"—I didn't want to say this next part, but I had to—"face-to-face. Do you want to drop by the house, say, sometime after dinner?" Kevin hated dogs and claimed he was allergic. I wouldn't vacuum before he came. Toby would be there to protect me.

"Information?" he asked. "Your place? Sounds like a plan. But before I see you on this *business*, there is something I need to say to you. Clear the air."

Here we go, I thought, already getting complicated. "Sure." I tried to sound indifferent, not easy, as it was not my normal state. "Let's hear it."

"I understand you didn't pass on my message to Darlene years ago, you know, that I wanted her back. I can't remember the details, doesn't matter anyway. I've been doing some heavy thinking. Reaching down and going deep." Kevin paused, awed by his own sensitivity. He sounded so happy, it worried me.

"Deep? What are you talking about?"

"What doesn't break you makes you stronger. Timing is everything." Kevin struggled to get the words out, as touched as he was by his wisdom. "Absence makes the heart grow fonder. Everything happens for a reason."

"Meaning?" I asked.

"I'm thinking the long and winding road might have brought me back to the love of my life," Kevin said. "And I owe it all to you."

I definitely wasn't vacuuming. I'd put the dog blanket from Toby's bed on the couch and make this man sit on it.

"Actually, that you're here you owe to a fire," I said. "That's all you and I have to talk about. See you at, say, seven?"

I wasn't sure Kevin heard me.

"From now on, Val," he said, "I'm going to stay on track and never look back. The Dalai Lama."

"Got that wrong, Kev. Dolly Parton."

I hung up.

CHAPTER TWENTY

Before I talked to Kevin, there was another other person I needed to see first.

Darlene.

Today was one of her regular days at the municipal offices. There, she'd be doing whatever deputy mayors did, which, as far as I knew, meant talking to people with concerns who wanted a more sympathetic ear than was on either side of Mayor Elliot Clark's head.

As I walked up the green linoleum tiled stairs to the second floor of the Drummond/Gasper's Cove municipal offices, I thought about the many transitions Darlene had made in her life. She'd come far, in a way that only women who had been underestimated could.

And it wasn't as if Darlene hadn't had previous moments of public recognition. All that had started in Grade Five, when she officially became the only girl in the school to wear a bra, one that was unpadded because that wasn't at all necessary. Possibly not unrelated, she had gone steady nonstop all the way through to graduation, George being the only boyfriend that, in my opinion, had been worth her time. That had been followed by a confusing period when she had managed to be known both as Gasper's Cove's best hairstylist (winner of the provincial Updo Championship, Eastern Shore Division, three years in a row) and the only woman in town who had survived not one but three inappropriate marriages. Not that people thought any of that was her fault. Darlene was generally considered to be a person good with hair, but bad with men, not something to be held against her. After all, no one could be excellent at everything.

What got missed in all those years of hairdressing and divorcing were the survival skills Darlene collected. Inside the head of her ever-changing hair colors was a mind that could think. And inside her heart was an ability to know how another person was feeling. As a result, it was no surprise to me that when she ran for office, she won by a landslide. Whatever the qualifications of her competitors, no one else had her goodwill. In a small town, if you dig yourself out in a snowstorm to go do the hair of someone's grandmother in hospital, it is remembered.

When I arrived at the door of her office, I caught Darlene in a moment of civic leadership.

"How's this for an idea?" she asked two middle-age ratepayers, one male and fastidious, one female and artsy. "You, Mr. MacIntyre, bring your dogs in during the full moon. And you," she said to a woman I recognized as a local knitter, "help your neighbor put down twigs or something crunchy at the edge of his flower beds. If your cats are like mine, they have fussy feet."

The combatants looked at each other.

"Seems unnecessary," the man identified as MacIntyre said, "but I could try it."

The knitter crossed her arms over her bosom. "If he stops that middle-of-the-night howling, I'll see what I can do about the cats in his garden."

"Great news," Darlene said. "I knew we could work something out." Her enthusiasm was not matched by her visitors. "Get back to me in a month. Tell me how it goes."

The knitter and MacIntyre nodded and, avoiding eye contact, trooped off down the stairs, each to go back to their own property and species.

"Enjoying yourself?" I asked Darlene.

"Loving it," she said. "Our mayor passes all the heavy conflict-resolution cases over to me, saves himself for the more delicate tasks, like the budget."

I followed Darlene into her office and sat down in the chair facing her desk. Darlene, to her credit, had done her best to spruce up the plain and worn civil service office. The louvered blinds on her window were now partially disguised by a pink and blue floral swag I had sewn for her. There were matching seat cushions on each of her three chairs, a vase of cut flowers from the Foodmart, framed pictures of all of her current and past cats, and a big, long photograph of our extended family, taken near the water, rows and rows of Rankin cousins and parents. Darlene's decor made her point: Being a city official, a deputy mayor, and a woman did not mean she had to hide who she was, it was an opportunity for her to demonstrate it. To herself and to the rest of us.

I sat in my chair and waited for Darlene to speak first. I felt there was an elephant in the room, and I'd seen his car parked outside Darlene's house. Kevin Johnson, the one person I had thought and hoped we would never see again, had returned. And I was sure he'd brought back with him what always had been his specialties: strife, division, and trouble.

"Val, I'm sorry I haven't been getting back to you. But I've been busy," Darlene said. Her face was bright. I knew that look. She had a secret to share.

"Busy doing what?"

Darlene leaned across her desk, folding her arms under the un-deputy-mayor-like cleavage of her crossover knit top. "Up to no good," she said. "Playing that man I was stupid enough to marry once. Look, he told me about that letter he wrote. He thought that bit of information would come between you and me. Shows how much he knows about how far I've come, who I really care about. He thought he was the one with unfinished business, but it was me who needed to settle things. For myself, for you, Val. So, I decided I needed to give him an overdue taste of his own medicine. And I've been enjoying the fact he's too stupid to know what I'm doing."

"What do you mean?"

"I just let that man talk. There's nothing he likes better than the sound of his own voice. And I found out a lot of very interesting things," she said, trying to stretch out the suspense, knowing she was annoying me.

"Like what?" I asked. Sometimes, my cousin was too much. "I called his dad's office, by the way. They were surprised he was here. What's he up to?"

"Where do I start?" Darlene asked. "First, Kevin's dad bailed him out and gave him a job when everything else he tried fell through. Big shocker. They started him out with office work. He messed that up. So, next, Kevin decided to make up a job for himself that would make use of his talents. He got it into his head he would be a crack insurance investigator, you know, uncover fraud. Because, well, who knows fraud better than Kevin? But he had to prove to his father he could do it. So, when the call came in about the fire here, and since Kevin knew the community, he grabbed the file and decided this was his chance."

"That explains something, I guess," I said. "But how is it going? Will he try to hold up the insurance claim?"

Darlene's confidence disappeared. She reached out to hold my hand. "It's a bit more than that," she said. "Don't freak out. But Kevin has this idea that the best way he can show his dad he's a great investigator is to not only find a fire that was started because of arson but also identify who the arsonist is. He has a couple of ideas. But the one he seems to be going with was that Chester lit the fire so he could collect this insurance money."

I thought my head was going to explode. This was exactly what I was afraid would happen. And now, it had. I let go of Darlene's hand and stood up, so quickly that I almost knocked over her vase of dyed carnations.

"No, no, no," I said, "what evidence does Kevin have? Specific evidence? Not everyone who has an insurance policy burns their place down. Most people don't. Particularly good, reasonable guys who used to be accountants. He has no proof that Chester is involved. And he can't have, because there's nothing there."

"I'm not sure he sees it that way," Darlene said. "He told me he's been reading up on burn patterns on the internet. Plus, he's got some insurance investigator's handbook, if you believe there's such a thing." She paused to rearrange the carnations and wipe some water off her desk, anything to avoid looking at me while she talked. "He mentioned something about an accelerant, whatever that is, and a trigger? And added to that is the fact Chester was in Gasper's the night before the fire. He was staying at Rollie's. Kevin also knows Chester left his job, and in his mind, that means he might need the money ..."

"Stop right there," I said. "I can explain most of this. Accelerant? I know what that is from the store. It means fuel. I happen to know that there was a stash of extremely flammable bootleg liquor hidden in that cottage. As for a trigger, look, Twyla was a medium, or thinks she was. The way I see it, she lit some mood candles for talking to old sailor ghosts and left them burning when she went to bed." I remembered the wine bottles in the blue recycling bag Tommy Hirtle had pointed out. "Or maybe she passed out in bed after she'd knocked over a candle, and it caught." I stopped to adjust the valance I'd made for the top of Darlene's window—the swag was crooked—and then continued. "I've got it all figured out. Kevin needs to know everything I told you. Chester had nothing to do with it."

"Hmm," Darlene said. "Not sure candles explain what he called a trigger. I understand they found the remnants of kind of a remote-control spark thing, you know, like they use to light BBQs, but on a remote control, when they went through the ashes. But you know Kevin. He could have been making that up just to sound dramatic. To me, a candle makes more sense." Darlene rearranged the pens and pencils in the mason jar on her desk. She loved to tidy. "But Twyla.

There's something else Kevin told me about her and Peter Tupper at the yacht club."

I held up my hand. "Stop. I know all about it. They used to work together in Halifax years ago. And they were married. But something happened, and they split up. I'm working on what brought them both here. I don't understand it."

"I do," Darlene said. "That's the interesting part. I knew they'd once been a couple, but that's not the point. It's the cottage. Yours. The one Twyla was staying in when it burnt down. Do you know who used to live there? The original owner, the old rumrunner? Kevin showed me the deed. You'll never guess whose great-grandfather he was."

Random bits of information ran toward each other in my head and joined hands.

"The original owner of the cottage, the rumrunner, was a man named Tupper. The same last name as Twyla's ex. Peter Tupper, a man from the city who also decided this was the summer to come to Gasper's Cove."

CHAPTER TWENTY-ONE

Darlene stared at me. "How did you know that?"

"My network," I said. "Some older ladies I know. That's not the point. A woman rents a cottage that once belonged to the family of her ex-husband and then dies in it. Anything that random has to mean something. Chester could be in trouble here, we've got to pay attention to everything."

"I agree," Darlene said. "Your kids are like my own kids. But what are we going to do?"

"Not sure. But I feel in my bones there is an answer to all this somewhere," I said. "My son didn't start any fires, that's not even worth talking about. We've got to point Kevin in another direction, and fast. The right direction."

"I'm with you," Darlene said. "This Tupper connection has to mean something important. But what? And how do we find out?"

"I don't have the answer to that," I admitted. "This is too much for my brain. We need someone logical, systematic, objective."

"Do we know anyone like that?" Darlene asked.

I did a quick mental scan of the population of Gasper's Cove, came up empty, then did a mental trip across the causeway to Drummond. I had my answer.

"Yes, I do," I said. "And I'm going to see him."

Darlene looked puzzled, then smiled. "You do that," she said. "In the meantime, what can I do?"

"What you should have done awhile ago," I said. "You've spent enough time lately with someone who never loved you. Go see someone who always has."

"Oh, dear," Darlene said. "You're right."

"You bet I am," I said. "You got some explaining to do. To the best Greek cook in this town."

The next morning, as I drove across to Drummond, it occurred to me I was better at understanding other people's relationships than my own. That is, if I had a relationship. I wasn't sure. After all, when I called Stuart's office, he suggested lunch. And then he said he wanted to talk to me, ask my advice, and give me a gift.

I had to admit to myself that our almost lunch date gave me conflicting emotions of both anticipation and anxiety. I had been the one to go to Stuart, for support and to access his steady common sense. The idea that he wanted to give me anything other than information, or that he needed my opinion, was a shift. I didn't know what it did, or didn't, mean.

When I arrived at the Chinese restaurant on the main floor below his office, Stuart was already there. I waved as I made my way over to our table, already set with a large heavy china teapot and two tiny cups for green tea. I noticed

Stuart had placed two envelopes, one large and brown, one small, white, and letter-size, underneath his cutlery and a paper sleeve of chopsticks.

He stood and pulled out a chair for me.

"I'm really glad you called," he said. "You beat me to it."

"No problem. I'm hungry too."

I looked at the envelopes. "I've got a complicated situation I need help sorting out, and you're good at that. But let's order. I can see what you want to show me first. That okay?"

Stuart snapped open one of the big plastic menus and handed it to me, then opened his own.

"Hot and sour soup?" he asked. He'd remembered what I'd ordered the last time we had eaten here together.

"Yes," I said. "But the bowls are huge. That and a couple of spring rolls should be enough."

"Same," Stuart said, signaling to the server. "Tea enough for you?" he asked, picking up the larger of the two envelopes. The sleeves of his dry cleaner–pressed cotton shirt were folded up to three-quarters length, exposing his muscular forearms and an elaborate watch like divers, or sailors, wore.

"Tea's fine," I said.

"Alrighty then." Stuart opened the envelope, extracted a yellowed sheet of heavy paper, and handed it over.

I was aware of his eyes on me as I looked at the drawing.

I knew immediately what it was.

"A sewing machine!" I said, reading the typed words at the top. *97. Revolving Hook Machines. Application filed May 5, 1913.* The delicate line drawing showed a view of a hand-wheel-driven domestic sewing machine, the side-loading bobbin case illustrated twice, once in place in the machine and once again in more detail near the bottom of the page, hand-labeled beautifully with long-forgotten skill as *Fig. 2, lines drawn to parts 20–50.*

"Amazing. This is hardly any different from the bobbin in my machine at home." I looked up at Stuart.

"I know," he said. "After I found this, I did a little research. Essentially, the modern rotating hook system is pretty much the same as the one Singer patented in 1851. Singer was quite a character. Twenty-six children, and he got a lot of his ideas from other inventors but was better at filing patents. What you are looking at here is a patent for one of the many variations of that original idea, developed for different machines for local manufacturers. This one was Canadian."

"Where did you get it?" To me, someone who had spent so much of her life in front of a sewing machine, this drawing was art.

"It was inside the drawers of an old map cabinet I got months ago at a government surplus auction. It's been in the garage. I had some idea of using it in the office for engineering drawings, but I couldn't get it to fit." Stuart said. "I grabbed the drawings for myself and donated it to the yacht club. Peter was very interested in it."

"I know. I was at the club, in the boathouse. I was there when he was refinishing it," I said. "Doing a careful job, as far as I could make out."

"Yes, it will look good in the clubhouse. He asked if there was anything inside when I bought it—must be as interested in technical drawings as I am. I think it came from the patent office; some of the drawings are mechanical and nautical. I'm planning on having them framed to put up in the office. I've got a thing for old documentation." He smiled. "But as soon as I saw this one, I knew it was for you."

"Thank you. Are you sure?" I was touched but couldn't find the words to express it. "An old patent like this might be valuable."

Stuart laughed. "I doubt it. I expect there are a lot of old sewing machine patents around. The only valuable ones would be those if the inventor, or invention, were well-known. But I knew this one would mean something to you, so I want you to have it. Now, what do you want to talk to me about?"

Our food arrived. I waited for the server to lower the plates of spring rolls and the oversize bowls of soup onto the table before I answered. I was unsure of where to start.

"Let's eat first," I said, picking up the little shovel of my china soup spoon. I noticed the second envelope on the table. I remembered that Stuart said he wanted my advice. "What's that?" I asked, unrolling my paper napkin and placing it on my lap.

"Ah, I've got a photo to show you," he said. "You have more experience than I do, and I'd appreciate your thoughts. It's taken me some time to get custody, but here he is." He pulled a photo out of the business envelope and slid it across the table to me.

"My boy."

He was adorable. Somewhere between six months and a year, it was hard to tell because he may have been small for his age, but he was alert, with intelligent eyes.

"Custody?" I asked. "What's the story there?"

Stuart sighed. "I was doing a job for an older gentleman who got him and then had to move. There was no one to take this little guy, so I asked the family if I could. It took a while to make the arrangements."

"Nova Scotia Duck Toller, isn't he?" I asked. "When do you get him?"

"Going to pick him up tomorrow," Stuart said. "His name is Birdie. I knew a wonderful border collie of that name when I was a kid. It's kind of like a sign."

Something about his tone of voice made me want to cry. Good dogs are never, ever, forgotten. "You haven't had a dog of your own before, have you?" I asked.

"No. When it was just me working a lot, and with Erin, I didn't feel I had the time. She's older now. But that's not it. I visited the dog at this man's son's house, and I knew. He was my dog. He was waiting for me. Does that sound nuts?"

"Not at all. Toby was a rescue, I feel the same way about him." I leaned back so the server could take our dishes. "What did you want to ask me?"

"I have to get ready," Stuart said. "What do I need?"

I made a list in my head. Duck Tollers were Nova Scotia's provincial dog, bred first in Yarmouth County at the south end of the province. They looked like little collies, but with a waterproof double coat. Any Duck Tollers I knew were bright, bouncy, smart dogs. And very loyal. I thought one would suit Stuart.

"You've already got what he needs most, all any dog really wants," I said. "A home. Someone they can rely on, someone they matter to. But apart from that, let's see. Good food." I pulled out a pen and an old receipt and wrote on it. "This is what I fed Toby at that age, but ask the vet too. If he doesn't have one, you'll need a nice dog bed, and I'd go for a good harness leash, something to chew on, and if he's skittish, you might try a crate, just at first, at night. See how he goes." I paused and considered. "I'd love to meet him."

"Oh, you will," Stuart said, lifting the teapot, holding onto the lid, even though it had been carefully secured to the handle with fishing line, to pour me a cup. "I was thinking maybe Birdie and I could meet you and Toby in the evenings to walk together?"

"That would be great," I said, lifting my cup and enjoying the aroma of jasmine and a suggestion of the future. "He'd love that." I paused. "And so would I. I've got one question, though. Something I've always wondered about. What's a Toller? What does that mean?"

"It's a way of hunting," Stuart said. "Most retrievers go after the birds, like what you'd expect from the name. But these dogs operate differently. The hunter sends them out as sort of decoys. *Tolling* means running around, playing, and distracting the ducks so the hunter can close in. Not that I'd ever hunt. Does that make sense?"

Something clicked into place. I could see the edges of a strategy.

"Oh, yes, it does," I said. "More than you know."

CHAPTER TWENTY-TWO

"What do you mean?" Stuart asked.

"It has to do with what I wanted to talk to you about. You've just given me a missing piece," I explained. "I thought what happened at our cottage had something to do with Twyla and Peter. They'd been married, and I thought that was important. It wasn't."

"I'm not following. How so?"

"It wasn't about them—thinking like that was like … tolling. A distraction. It was about the place. Their shared background, from work. There was something here in Gasper's Cove that they were both searching for."

"Like what?" Stuart asked. "I don't get it."

I leaned over and almost spilled my tea.

"It has to do with the department they both worked in, in government. Regulations. I know Twyla could get into Peter's email, his records. He was her husband after all, anything he knew, she knew too. That's how she sold him out incidentally, maybe to take his job for herself. I heard there was a woman involved. She must have accessed information on what he was up to when he was supposed to be working. His own research. His family originally came from around here. He must have heard things and was checking them out. It wasn't about zombie laws." Stuart looked mystified, and I couldn't blame him. "I'll explain that some other time. It had to do with all the ships that went down off this coast."

"Okay, I can follow that part," Stuart said carefully. "Nova Scotia has thousands of shipwrecks in our waters. But how does that fit with what you're saying?"

"What is the other thing we are known for around here?" I asked. "In our past, I mean. Besides shipwrecks?"

Stuart shrugged. "Lobster?"

"No. Think back. Rumrunners. All the men who used to bootleg booze down to the States during Prohibition. Lots of hidden coves, secrets, hideaways." I took a breath. "In fact, our cottage, the one that burned down? It was built by a rumrunner, a Tupper, one of Peter's relatives, I bet. There even was a stash of old liquor in it. I just found out about it. But that's not my point." I looked around, but the other diners close to us seemed busy wrestling with chopsticks. "Shipwrecks, treasure, rumrunners sneaking around looking for places to hide things. What if one of those rumrunners found something valuable, a treasure, you know how there's always rumors, and it got put away ..."

The light went on in Stuart's eyes. It made them look even bluer, brighter. I looked away. Eyes like that, a man like this, could break your heart, and you'd never get over it. I forced myself to continue.

"And Peter came here, maybe he heard something growing up, and he came back to find it. And Twyla came here to try and get to it first?" Stuart asked.

"Exactly, you got it." I was impressed. "That's why this séance nonsense. It gave her an excuse to go and look through old houses, to ask locals to talk about dead relatives, and to hear old stories. It was a cover, she was searching."

"It's a crazy idea," Stuart said, "but it makes sense." His face clouded. "But Twyla died. You don't suppose that wasn't an accident, do you? That maybe she found whatever it was, or was about to, and someone stopped her? How would that work?"

"I talked to Darlene," I said. "She told me that Kevin thinks that the fire was deliberately set, and he has evidence. They found something when they went through the site, a remote-control starter. Might have been there to start the fire." I looked at Stuart. "You're an engineer. What can you tell me about those things?"

Stuart shrugged. "These days, you can pretty much start anything from a distance. Something that would ignite, make a spark, would be easy to set up. All you need is a sender and a receiver."

"Give me an example."

"Car starters, televisions, a lot of electronics, drones ..."

"Stop right there," I ordered. Our server advanced with the bill, put it down, and, sensing a serious conversation, scurried away. That woman would need a good tip. "Did you say *drones*?"

"Yes, I did," Stuart said. "Look, even kids' toys these days can be run by remotes. Does it matter?"

"Oh, it does," I said. I opened my purse and slapped two twenties onto the table. I picked up the brown envelope and pushed my chair back. Stuart dropped his napkin onto the table and stood up. On an impulse, I reached over and kissed his cheek.

"Stuart," I said. "I love you. You're a genius." I knew who had started that fire at the cottage. And that meant I also had evidence that my son hadn't.

Stuart reached for me. I took a step backward. In my mind, I was already out the door.

"I'll catch you later," I said. "Right now, I'm off to talk to a creep."

As I walked away, I thought I heard Stuart call out something behind me, but I couldn't slow down to hear what it was. I had to talk to Kevin and explain everything. This couldn't wait for a house visit. I needed to see him now. I called Kevin's number, but all I got was a message that his mailbox was full.

I had to track him down. He wasn't answering his cell phone. Maybe he was at his motel. It was mid-afternoon. Kevin struck me as the kind who took naps in the middle of workdays. I dialed the motel's number and waited.

"Anchor Motel and Convention Center," a raspy voice said, then coughed.

"Kevin Johnson, please. I don't know his room number. Can you connect me?"

The man on the phone cleared his throat. "Will do. Here you go now."

My lucky day. Kevin was in.

"Valerie, my girl. A blast from the past. I was just thinking of you," Kevin crooned. I thought I heard ice cubes clinking in a glass in the background.

I forced a smile into my voice. "What a coincidence," I said. "I was passing by. Hoped I would catch you. Do you mind if I pop by? Love to have a chat." I mimed a gag in the rearview mirror, for my own benefit, if no one else's. It made me feel better.

"Room 313," Kevin said, as if he was ordering pizza delivery. "I'll be waiting for you, Valerie. Like I have been for years."

"Business," I said. "This is strictly business."

The ice cubes clinked again. "That's what they all say, kid." I could hear the smirk. "That's what they all say."

CHAPTER TWENTY-THREE

The door of room 313 was ajar when I arrived. I wasn't surprised to hear the strains of Dean Martin's "Everybody Loves Somebody" spilling out onto the fuchsia swirls cut into the broadloom in a previous decade. The hallway carpet, like Kevin himself, was a leftover from another era in taste.

Tentatively, I pushed the door open. Inside, leaning against the doorway of the motel bathroom, either for effect or support, one leg crossed over the other, one hairy, gold-linked braceleted arm in full view, was a man Darlene had married in a period of her life when she was too inexperienced to know what she did now. Kevin hadn't updated at all. Everything that had made him seem sophisticated when Darlene and I were so young aged Kevin now.

"Hey, gorgeous," Kevin smiled, "just in time for cocktail hour." He tossed his head toward the top of the minibar beside the bed. He had thoughtfully laid out a glass for me, next to a folded, stiff version of a hand towel he had borrowed from the bathroom, beside a display of tiny liquor bottles. "Take your pick."

I was suddenly hit with an intense wave of longing for Stuart, jasmine tea, and talk about dogs.

"No thanks," I said. There was nowhere to sit. The room held only one chair, burgundy, polyester damask, spotted with historic cigarette burns, and draped with a satin dressing gown with a large dragon on the back. I stayed standing.

"I have information for you about the fire at our cottage," I said.

The expression in Kevin's eyes shifted, from one kind of calculation to another.

"You've been talking to the ex-wife, haven't you?" he said. "Who, by the way, isn't my type anymore. This deputy mayor thing has gone to her head. But that's neither here nor there, water under the bridge. Moved on to bigger and better things myself."

"Good for you," I said, determined to have the conversation I had come to have. "About the fire. I know who did it."

"Do you now?" Kevin sneered. "More likely you've come here to do the hysterical mother bit and tell me your precious baby boy didn't do it. Too late for that."

He didn't have that part completely wrong, but I did have evidence, or at least a very strong theory, which, in my mind, was the same thing. "What do you mean 'too late'?" I asked.

Kevin reached over and raised one of the little bottles. Rum. I shook my head. He unscrewed the tiny cap and poured the contents into his glass.

"Us investigators put together puzzles. All the pieces fit with this one. Number one, CJ took out the policy, his signature is first. His brother and sister signed it later. Number two, the kid's out of a job. We all know that causes cash-flow issues." Kevin swirled his rum and ice. "Number three, he was in the vicinity. Ran into a guy afterward, at the fire site, one of the volunteers, he came back to check on things, and I caught him when I was leaving. I can get him on the record saying CJ was in Gasper's the night of the fire." Kevin took a deep sip of his drink and then raised his glass. "Bingo, we've got a winner. Wait 'til I tell the old man this one."

I tried to control the impulse to walk out of this tired motel room with this retread of a man. I had to stay. What Kevin said didn't look good, I admitted that, I'd been expecting it. Darlene and I had gone over this. But Kevin had left out the most important part of the equation, and that was the piece I had.

"Coincidence," I said. "Having an insurance policy doesn't make anyone an arsonist. Chester wasn't the only person in Gasper's Cove that night. But you are forgetting something. A deliberately lit fire doesn't start itself. I heard you found something at the cottage."

Kevin was no longer smiling. "Me and my big mouth," he said. "I knew I should never have gone to see Darlene. But you're not as smart as you think you are, either of you. You forget, I've known CJ a long time. I was around for a bit when he was a kid."

"What is that supposed to mean?"

"He and his brother had those little cars. Remember? They used to race them on the street." Kevin crossed his arms across his chest. I saw the glint of a heavy gold chain in the open neck of his shirt.

I stared at him. "He was five or six when he did that!" I couldn't believe this guy. "Every kid in town had one of those cars. What are you thinking? He saved a toy from his childhood to set fire to his own cottage twenty years later? You're making a fool of yourself."

I had touched a nerve. An old and frayed one.

"Course not," Kevin said. "I'm just saying he knew the technology. Been upgraded, for sure. And after all, look where he came from: Toronto. You can get anything in a city like that."

I picked up the acetate satin robe from the chair carefully, touching only the lapel, and threw it on the quilted cover of the motel room bed. I sat down, too tired to keep standing.

"Enough of this. Look, there is someone else you need to look at. There's a far bigger picture here that you know nothing about."

Kevin snorted. "Like what?"

"You and Darlene aren't the only exes in the situation. Peter at the yacht club used to be married to Twyla, the woman who died. That old cottage, like a lot of them around here, was built by a rumrunner. Peter's great-grandfather. You know what local guys in those days were up to, lots of secrets, they were in and out of places in the water no one else was." The word *secrets* had caught Kevin's attention. I knew the direction to take to keep his interest. "You know the stories about shipwrecks and treasures, we all do. People have been up and down this coast for years trying to find them." I took note of a dim light that went on in Kevin's eyes at the mention of *treasure*.

"Go on," he said.

"Peter came back here for a reason, maybe something his rumrunner great-grandfather told the family, I don't know." I had another flash of inspiration. "And he might not have been the only one looking. I mean, Harry used a drone to fly along the coast. Twyla maybe was another one. She knew about legislation governing what you could take from shipwrecks. I think she might have been getting close, too, even found something. Maybe someone knew where she was staying, staged the fire to get rid of her. You already found the way they did it."

Kevin's eyes were moving back and forth in his head, almost as if he were watching a race. I knew this meant he was thinking. The possibility he was in the vicinity of treasure had diverted his attention.

"Way?" he asked, distracted. "What way?"

"You're not much of a listener, are you?" I asked him. "I just told you. Drones. Harry's is at the boat club. I saw it on the workbench. Anyone could get it. Those things run on a remote, like the kids' cars. Like lighters. Harry does odd jobs around the community. Both Peter and Tommy Hirtle were in the cottage. It's possible someone started the fire and didn't know the place had 100-proof bootleg booze in the walls, or that the fire would go so fast, the smoke would kill her before she had a chance to get out."

Kevin put down his glass and studied the dark screen of the huge television mounted on the wall, as if it would suddenly turn itself on and show him some answers.

"You're saying this might all be about something from one of the old shipwrecks? And treasure hunters?"

"Yes. You got it. Finally."

Kevin started to hum along with Dean Martin. "I'm thinking Oak Island, other places, along the coast where they talked about hidden treasure ... they say there's a fortune." His eyes focused on me. "If either of these two found something, it would be worth a lot."

"I suppose it could be," I said.

Kevin reached over to the bedside table, picked up a worn and stuffed leather wallet, and shoved it into the back pocket of his pants.

"Drone, you say? The boathouse at the yacht club? Good place to keep things." Kevin walked to the door and held it open. "Thanks for coming by, Val. My instinct told me that this file was still open. Not every stone had been unturned. I was going to go over and talk to the boys at the club anyway, they were on my list all along. Better sooner than later, strike while the iron's hot, so to speak."

"Glad I was some kind of help," I said, walking through the door, wishing Kevin would move aside to give me more room. "You're the pro."

As I walked down the swirly carpet toward the door to the outside and fresh air, I was aware of Kevin's eyes on me.

"Hey, Val," he called out. "You still got it. And don't let anyone tell you differently."

CHAPTER TWENTY-FOUR

After I left all my theories and worries in Kevin Johnson's incapable hands, I went home and took Toby out for a walk. We were at the end of the street, halfway back from the field at the elementary school, when my phone rang.

It was Colleen.

"Everything okay at the store?" I asked. "I had to see someone, I'm walking Toby, but I can come in."

"No, we're fine," Colleen said. "A couple of the girls are upstairs, taking care of the Co-op; Duck and I've got the main floor covered. It's late, we'll be closing soon anyway. It's not that. It's my mother."

"Bernadette?" I asked. "Is everything alright? I just saw her."

"No, my mother's in great shape, probably going to outlive the rest of us. It's not that. She called the store today. She wants you to go out and see her, in private."

"Really? In private? What about?"

"No idea, my mother's life isn't that complicated, but she sounded worried. She wanted to know if you could go there this evening. Do you think you can do that?" Colleen asked. "It's probably some little thing."

"I'm almost at the house," I said. "I'll take Toby in, then jump in the car. Can you get in touch with your mom and let her know I am on my way?"

And I was.

The woman at the desk was one I didn't know.

"Here to see a resident?" she asked. "Dinner's over. Most of them are upstairs. Do you want me to call someone and let them know you are here?"

"Not to worry," I said. "I'll just run up. I know where I'm going." The receptionist waited for more information, but I gave her none.

I took the stairs so I wouldn't run into anyone I knew. Bernadette wanted to talk to me alone; I had no idea why. Her small apartment was at the back, #210, overlooking the trees, on the side away from the water. Outside her door, Bernadette had placed a small table, and on it, a frog held a bouquet on top of a crocheted doily she had probably made herself.

I knocked and waited. On the other side of the door, I heard the television turn off and the soft shuffle of foam-tread slippers on the parquet wood floor. The door opened, the unused chain rattling on its edge. Bernadette beamed when she saw me. She was dressed for visitors, a cherry-colored cardigan over a small print navy blouse, and clip-on button earrings on her ears.

"Valerie? Thank you for coming by tonight. I've got chair yoga in the morning," she said. "Hope it didn't put you out to pop over."

"No, not at all. Always happy to see you." I stepped into a tiny vestibule. "I hear there is something you wanted to talk about."

"Yes, there is. Come in." Bernadette opened the door wider. "I'll make us tea."

I followed Bernadette into her small living room and sat down on an armchair. It had crochet covers on its arms and two granny square afghans folded over its back. Before she'd come here, Bernadette had lived in a two-story house not far from the causeway. She'd been there for sixty years, married, mothered, and widowed there. As far as I could tell, nearly all of its contents had come to this small apartment with her. The perimeter of the room was ringed with armchairs, in rows, like an antiques dealer's rendition of a waiting room. I counted at least seven tiny tables, each with its own African violet, and a corner china cabinet from pre–Great War days crammed with stacks of gold-rimmed dinner plates, three silver tea services, and dozens of teacups stacked like filigree leaning towers of Pisa.

All the walls and every available horizontal surface were covered in family photos.

Bernadette sat down next to me. "I might as well get it over with. This thing has been a burden to me for so many years. I'd like you to help me."

"Whatever you need," I said.

Bernadette hesitated, then seemed to make up her mind.

"Here it is." She reached between us to a standing sewing basket, its wicker-wrapped wire legs raising it to sock-darning and mending height. She lifted the lid and reached down deep into it, working her way through ancient spools of thread and paper packets of sewing needles. "There's a storage place underneath here," she said, her fingers feeling for something she couldn't see. She stopped when she had it.

She passed me a package. "Open it," she said.

The package in my lap was wrapped in thick heavy paper, tied up in a bow with rickrack. This, I untied. I spread the paper open like a nest around what my seamstress's eyes knew immediately was tulle.

"A veil," I said. "A bride's veil. Whose is it? Yours?"

"I wish," Bernadette said. "Which I guess is the point. We didn't have that kind of money when I got married. I wore a street dress and a little hat. I told my mother that was exactly what I wanted. But it wasn't. I always wished I'd had a satin dress and a veil." She reached out a blue-veined hand and stroked the fine netting as tenderly as if it were a baby's cheek. "Like this one. Which is why I took it."

"Excuse me?"

"That night, when the girls and I went into Drysdale's, I saw it behind the glass under the counter. It was with the appliqués. White and ivory. Sequins and little pearls sewn on them. Fancy, expensive. This veil was laid out on display. Like a fairy cloud. So light." Bernadette spoke not to me but to the veil, her confidante from the past, the one who had been with her then and understood. "When Minnie and Joyce were carrying things out, I grabbed the veil and put it into my bag. I was a married woman then. No need for it. I was afraid if the other two saw it, they'd want to give it to some young woman. And I wanted it for myself."

"It's been in the bottom of your sewing basket all this time?" I asked.

"Yes, it has," Bernadette said. "But I wanted to wrap it up to keep it safe. That liquor we found hidden in that place in the cottage, it was wrapped in old paper. I grabbed some, wrapped it around the veil, and snuck it into the house." Bernadette lifted her hand and looked at me. "I know what you're thinking: Why didn't I tell them?"

"I am sure they would have understood," I said. "They were your friends." And, I wanted to say, you had already stolen together. What's one veil among thieves?

"Yes, they were," Bernadette said. "But this was something for me. Something special. I was one of fifteen children. My dad was on the boats," she added, so I would understand. "All this about the past coming back now. I needed to talk. To you. In private."

"I understand," I said, because I did. "Some things, after a while, you just don't want to keep to yourself." I realized I was talking about myself, and maybe Stuart.

"You're right about that," Bernadette sighed. "You keep a secret too long, it goes bad, however innocent it was to start with. But that's not all of it. There is something I need you to do for me."

"Anything," I said, wrapping the stolen veil up in its covering, retying the rickrack in a bow. I handed it to Bernadette. "Here it is."

"No," she said. "You keep it. I want Darlene to have it, to wear at her wedding to George. Those Greek weddings are fancy. I want to do her proud. There's only one thing."

"What's that?" I asked.

"Please don't tell her where it came from," Bernadette asked. "Make up something believable."

"I'll come up with an idea," I said, "Don't you worry about it."

Bernadette smiled and leaned back in her chair.

"Maybe just one more secret," she said. "Do you think if it's for a good cause, it won't count?"

CHAPTER TWENTY-FIVE

The stolen veil lay on the passenger seat beside me, tied up like a gift. I thought of Bernadette, years ago, the otherwise responsible, respectable wife and mother who had not been able to resist it. The tulle used to make veils like this one was so much finer than anything sold today. I undid the rickrack and unwrapped the paper for one more look.

There it was, a gossamer cloud, just as Bernadette had described it, gathered into an arc covered with pearls and sprigs of wax baby's breath, set onto a large comb. In the early sixties, when the veil was made, it had been designed to accent an updo or bubble hairstyle and be the star of the show. But this veil had not had its chance. Instead, it had spent the prime of its life wrapped in old paper at the bottom of a sewing basket. If Darlene wore it, it could complete its cycle. I started to wrap the tulle for delivery, then stopped.

The paper it was wrapped in was, in fact, three smaller sheets of paper, overlapped to cover their treasure. One of the sheets had something drawn on it. I pulled it out and spread it on my lap. On it was an ink drawing. Scrolled at the top were the words *"Yet another great new invention of F.W.B."*

A spark went off in some remote compartment of my mind. One of these words mattered. I didn't know which. I scanned the drawing below.

It was crude, like something someone had done quickly and passed over to a colleague, like a note you would scrawl in a meeting to make them laugh. It was a caricature in four parts. As far as I could make out, it showed a man straddling what looked like a sort of torpedo, then shot into the air, landing on the water, and then nose-diving under the waves. At the bottom was written *To be continued ... Nov. 19, 1921.* It was signed *H.A.L.*

I didn't know what I was looking at, but I knew somehow that it was important. What if all of this had nothing to do with shipwrecks? Was this the treasure Twyla Waters had been looking for? Was this why she had died?

If it was, then I had a good idea who had killed her.

I wondered if Stuart Campbell was at home.

As I drove to Stuart's house in Drummond, I rolled up the car window. The ocean air cooled quickly once the sun slid down below the horizon. Up in the sky, I heard honking. A big V of Canada geese was in flight, on their way out of Gasper's, starting the long journey south for the winter. They flew in a tight, purposeful formation, as if they were travelers late for some late-arrival check-in. This made me wonder, where did geese sleep at night? Or Tommy's raccoons? Where did they go after he had chased them away with the cultural programming? And come to think of it, what kind of a mind did that man have? To be able to devise such a humane way to chase away ring-eyed, ring-tailed invaders, but at the same time, to have no control over an impulse to steal? How many layers were there in people? How many had secrets? Who else was not who they seemed?

And who, in 1920, were F.W.B. and H.A.L.?

That cartoon, the script and the ink lines, reminded me of the sewing machine patent Stuart had given me. If anyone knew what this cartoon meant, it would be him. I pulled up in front of his house. It was nearly eight. I wondered if it was too late to visit. But the lights were on. I walked up to the door and knocked.

There was no answer.

I knocked again and waited. Erin was still away at camp. I wondered if Stuart had picked up his new dog. A high-pitched bark from down the street gave me my answer.

Walking toward me was a small busy dog. The little Duck Toller saw me and pulled on the leash in Stuart's hand. As they came closer, I saw a small sharp face, like a fox, framed by a ruff of auburn fur.

"Hey, Birdie," Stuart called out from the other end of the leash. "Slow down. Loose leash, take it easy, relax, man." They reached the end of the walkway that turned from the sidewalk to the house. The dog responded to Stuart's instructions by pulling on the leash even harder, his bright brown eyes intent on reaching me as quickly as possible.

"Well, now you've met Birdie," Stuart said. "I've never owned a dog before. I'm not sure *owned* is the right word. I think we've got a way to go. I've been reading books and listening to dog-training podcasts, but I don't think Birdie has."

I bent down for a closer look at the little dog's face and fell in love.

"He's a doll," I said, putting my package down on the steps so I could get both my hands into the red fur. "What a beautiful, beautiful baby."

I noticed Stuart had on plaid flannel pants and a T-shirt. I'd never seen him in anything but a buttoned-up shirt before. "He is, isn't he? Lovely boy, even though neither of us know what we're doing."

"How's the food going?" I asked, straightening up.

"No complaints there. Eats well. Both from the bowl and from my sports coat. I had a handful of kibble in a pocket, and he ate right through the jacket to get to it."

"Hmm," I said. "Let me have a look at it later. Maybe I can mend it. Exercise? Housetraining?"

"That's one thing we've got under control," Stuart said. "I get up early and let him out, get dressed, and we walk. That's his outdoor exercise. If you stay long enough, you can see him do the circuit around the living room. Along the couch, back of the chairs, with the grand finale, a flying leap across the coffee table."

"So, he's nimble," I said. I was aware of a small tongue delicately licking the back of my knee. "How about nights? Is he sleeping in the crate?"

Stuart laughed, the corners of his eyes creasing. Why did women worry about wrinkles? They made men more attractive.

"We tried that," he said. "But he whimpered something terrible in there. I couldn't stand it."

I knew how to translate this. "He slept with you."

"On and off," Stuart said. "Fair bit of horsing around. When I woke up, his head was inside the pillowcase beside me. One word of advice: If you get a Duck Toller? Forget the goose-down pillows." Stuart stopped and looked at the parcel on the steps. "But you didn't just come here to do a dog check, did you? What's up?" Stuart opened his front door, gently undid the leash from Birdie's collar, and ushered us both into the house.

"I have sort of a crazy idea, and I've found something here"—I picked up the veil wrapped in its paper—"that might be in the middle of it. But I need your opinion."

Stuart reached over me to close the door. With his hand still on the door jam near my shoulder, he studied my face.

"How about I put the kettle on and you tell me what this is about?" he said.

For the first time in a while, I felt relief. I'd come to the right person for help.

CHAPTER TWENTY-SIX

The tea was lemon ginger. I sat at Stuart's kitchen table, watching Birdie in a dog bed in the corner, pretending to gnaw at a dog bone but only using this as a disguise while he assessed me.

I, in turn, made small talk while I assessed the man at the kitchen counter carefully arranging peach and ginger muffins on a plate.

"Erin back from camp soon?" I asked. "School will be starting next week, won't it?"

"Yes, it will, and yes, she's back tomorrow. That's why I've been cooking. This is the second summer she's gone to camp. She loves it. But she's excited to come home and meet our dog." There was a wistfulness in Stuart's voice. He walked over, put the plate on the table, and sat down. I immediately put one of the muffins on my plate. Stuart was a wonderful baker and an excellent cook. I surveyed the kitchen. Marigolds were in a "World's Greatest Dad" mug on the counter. The tea towels on the handle of the oven door had been bought at the Crafters' Co-op. The dish detergent was expensive and eco-friendly. A weekly menu, printed in round, slightly backhand engineer's script, was on the fridge, attached at all four corners by magnets shared with a crooked letter, signed by Erin, a tiny heart drawn as a dot on the "I." The calendar on the wall was one sent when a person donated to Guide Dogs for the Blind. A brand-new backpack and a new water bottle waited on the seat of a chair pushed up to a pink and purple laminated placemat.

Stuart caught my eye and smiled. He knew exactly what I was thinking. "When you're the only parent, you try to be everything they need."

"I understand, completely," I said. "Feeling responsible for them never stops."

"What do you mean?"

"It's the real reason I'm here," I said. "Kevin, that insurance guy you've met, you're right, he thinks our fire was arson. And"—it was hard to get the next words out—"Chester is his most likely suspect."

Stuart reached over and patted the top of Birdie's head so he wouldn't have to look at me while he decided what to say.

"You've got to understand, Val, he has to look at all the possibilities. The name on the policy, the only Canadian resident, is the logical place to start." Stuart handed Birdie a yak bone to chew on and turned around to me. "And when he finds out there's nothing there, he'll move on."

I tried to keep my voice calm, the volume level. "Here's the thing. It's been clear to me for a while that if there was another person with a good motive for starting the fire, the focus would be off Chester. Then, my kids would get the insurance and rebuild, and they will keep coming back here every summer." I kept going. "Then, Kevin would leave town, this time for good. And George and Darlene would get married, and she would wear this beautiful veil her grandmother stole." I reached over to the parcel and untied the rickrack. I carefully took out the tulle and laid it on the table. Then, I spread out the cartoon, smoothing the decades-old creases with my hands. "Kevin knows what I think. But I need evidence. I wonder if this could be it, because, well, it's so old."

"I understand only half of what you just told me," Stuart said. "Maybe only 30 percent, tops, more like 25 percent." He stopped talking, riveted by the drawing on the table. "What's that?"

"This is what I am trying to explain. Maybe the key to this whole mess. You know about these things. That's why I'm here."

"Gee, and I thought you were here for the muffins," Stuart said, gently reaching for the drawing to turn it around and study it.

"Where did you get this?" He whistled. "Do you have any idea what it is?"

Had I heard a note of respect in his voice? Or was I searching for it?

"The veil was wrapped up in it, put away for a long time. I think that the paper came from our old cottage, the one the Tuppers built originally. This drawing reminded me of that sewing machine diagram you gave me and what you said about these things sometimes being valuable." Stuart kept his eyes on the cartoon, but I knew he was listening. "What do you think it is? Looks to me like pictures of some kind of torpedo, but look at the date."

Stuart pulled a pen out of his pocket and used it to point out details on the yellowed sheet, as if he was afraid to touch it with his hands.

"The title," he said. "Invention and F.W.B. I've seen something like this before in the museum in Baddeck. Those were the initials of Frederick Walker Baldwin. You've probably heard of him. Casey Baldwin. Alexander Graham Bell's protege. The first Canadian to fly an airplane, the man who came up with the first design for the hydrofoil, later member of the legislature for Victoria and founder of Cape Breton Highlands National Park."

Casey Baldwin? Where had I heard that name recently? "And the initials at the end?" I asked. "After the date?"

"H.A.L.?" Stuart smiled. "That stands for H.A. Largelamb, something Bell used to call himself as a joke. And these drawings." Stuart's pen tapped the page again, four times, one for each step. "If I'm not mistaken, these aren't pictures of a torpedo, as you called it, but drawings of Baldwin's first iteration of the hydrofoil."

"Would that make it valuable?" I asked Stuart.

"If it is an original, and it looks like it is, I'd say yes," Stuart said. "But where did it come from? Before it became wrapping paper, I mean."

I didn't say anything. I sipped my tea. I felt like there was a curtain in the back of my mind and behind it was a tiny missing piece like a back neck facing that would make sense of it all. In the corner, Birdie dropped the bone hard on the floor. He leaned out of his bed to retrieve it.

"That's one gorgeous dog," I said, distracted. "Erin is going to be so happy when she meets him."

Stuart leaned down and stroked the little dog's head. "You're a pretty boy," he cooed. He looked up at me. "Official dog of Nova Scotia," he said. "In 1995, the legislature passed something called the Provincial Dog Act."

The curtain moved aside. Just a little. "The legislature?" I asked. "The same one where the famous Casey Baldwin was a Member of the Legislative Assembly? The kind of big name that if you were a candidate running in a small constituency, you'd be pretty pleased to have come down to canvass for you? An outdoorsman, a guy who founded a huge provincial park, someone you'd put up in a beautiful cottage on the coast when he stayed?"

"I'm not keeping up here," Stuart said. "What are you talking about?"

I could see it all now. "I got tolled with the vintage knick-knacks. Then, with the idea of ghosts, treasures, and zombies. But it wasn't about any of that. It was about this." I tapped on the drawing. "Someone who heard the stories growing up and told his ex-wife. Someone who came back here to find their roots and this drawing. Why didn't I see it before?" I stared at Stuart. "It was the ears. I should have put it all together."

"Ears?" Stuart asked.

"Big ones," I said. "Runs in the family. That branch of the Tuppers all have them."

CHAPTER TWENTY-SEVEN

"Are you talking Tupper as in Peter from the yacht club?" Stuart stood up and brought the teapot to the table. "I think you're going to have to give me more detail."

"It was the ladies at Seaview Manor who told me," I explained. "Years ago, in the 1930s, a local man of that name ran for the provincial legislature. Casey Baldwin, who was famous for the Bell connection and a member of the legislature himself, came here to campaign for this Tupper. Who lost, but that's not the point."

"Keep going."

"I wonder if Baldwin brought this"—I pointed to the cartoon—"with him. It was a novelty, it was funny, and maybe reinforced a time that was the best years of his life. I don't know. At any rate, I have an idea that somehow, the drawing got left here, or was taken, and the Tupper family put it away. I think Peter might have heard about this growing up, mentioned it to Twyla, and they both came back here, on their own, to find it. Of course, neither of them was successful because the Alexander Graham Bell cartoon had been retired to the bottom of a sewing basket years ago."

"You do know that there's a big gap here, don't you?" Stuart asked. "Between two people looking for the same valuable document and one of them ending up dead."

"I got an answer for that," I said, holding up my phone. "Chester's reservations. Twyla changed hers at the last minute. She arrived a day early at the cottage. That fire was deliberately lit by someone who had a remote control, the kind Peter knew about from the drone. He was getting tired of her hanging around, the woman who had taken his job, maybe broken his heart. He wanted his own past back, he wanted to stay in the cottage because it had once been in his family. He even tried to rent it long-term, but my kids couldn't commit to that. And then Twyla showed up looking to beat him to the Bell cartoon. I think he'd had enough. When precise people blow, they really blow. I know that, I've been setting them off my whole life. Back to my theory. It makes sense. Every time Peter had something, Twyla took it away from him. She was even staying in a home he couldn't get back for himself. Peter played by the rules, Twyla didn't. It wasn't fair. If he couldn't have that cottage, he wanted to make sure no one did. And he wanted her gone. So, he burned it down, with her in it."

"You're talking murder, not an accident," Stuart said. "A person would have to be pretty unbalanced to do something like that."

"This is a man who lost a good civil service job because he was trying to get the federal government to take a law banning water-skiing at night from the books," I said. "And other zombies."

Stuart picked up a napkin and wiped a muffin crumb from my mouth. "If there's even a small chance you're right about this, there's only one thing to do now."

"Go to the RCMP," I said, finishing the sentence for him. "So they can grab Peter before he can get away."

Stuart wanted to drive, but I wouldn't let him. I felt that since I'd done all the figuring out, I should be the one to explain it to Wade. Stuart still wanted to come with me, and I was glad he did. In a supporting role.

As it turned out, explanations and support weren't necessary.

We had our hands on the big glass doors of the Royal Canadian Mounted Police detachment in Drummond when the door swung open, hitting me in the face. If Stuart hadn't caught me, it could have knocked me flat.

"Hey, Harry," Stuart said. "You might want to be more careful."

It was then I noticed the van in the parking lot at the side of the building, *Odd Job Harry*. "Latest enterprise," Harry said, following my gaze. "By popular demand, a bit of a moneymaker between shifts at the club."

I rubbed my forehead, wondering if I would have a bruise. "Doing odd jobs for the Mounties?" I asked.

"Nah, nothing like that," he said. "Making a statement. Kind of an eyewitness to the explosion."

"Explosion?" Stuart asked. "What do you mean?"

"Haven't heard yet?" Harry asked, smoothing his comb-over to cover a sunburned spot on the back of his head. "I expect I'll be doing interviews. Good thing I know how to handle the media."

"Go back a bit," Stuart said. "There was an explosion?"

"Yup, down at the yacht club," Harry said, drawing himself up to his full height, even with Stuart's chin. "The entire boathouse. Whole shooting match. Kaboom. Something set off the propane tanks inside. Found what was left of one in the yard myself. Safety valve had been turned off."

"No way," Stuart said. "Anyone hurt?"

"Hurt? I'll say. Peter was inside when it went off. Bad news." Harry shook his head. "Makes no sense. Good thing Tommy Hirtle was there."

"Tommy? What does he have to do with it?" I asked. "More important, is Peter alright?"

"Yes and no," Harry said. "Good and bad. The good thing was that the big doors to the dock were open. I guess the blast sent Peter flying right over the rollers and out into the water. That's the good part."

"And the bad part?" Stuart said, evenly. I could tell he wanted to shake the information out of Harry, not that that would have done much good.

"Old Peter can't swim," Harry explained. "At least not under pressure. I mean, it was like he was shot out of a cannon, even left that mustache behind. Not a hair of it left. Those fancy things take awhile to grow," Harry stroked his own long upper lip. "Don't have the patience myself."

"Harry," Stuart said slowly, "what happened?"

"I just told you, Tommy was there, picking something up, and he can move fast for an old guy, I can tell you that. Tommy jumped into a dinghy and pulled Peter out of the water with a boat hook." For once, Harry seemed impressed by someone other than himself. "Once a fisherman always a fisherman, I guess."

"So, where's Peter now?" I asked.

"Drummond Consolidated," Harry said. "The hospital. The ambulance came right quick. Hopefully when they put something over the place where the mustache was and pump the seawater out of him, he'll be good to go." Harry's pocket started to play the *Star Wars* theme. "Excuse me," he said, pulling out his phone. "Hey, Mom ... a quart of milk on the way home? Eggs? Sure thing." He looked at Stuart and me, winked, and mouthed *my mother*. "What's for dinner? Meatloaf? On my way. Got to go folks," he said, sliding the phone back into his pocket. "Duty calls. Smell you later."

Stuart and I stepped away from the front door to let Harry amble off to his van.

"What do we do now?" I asked. "Another fire? At the boathouse? And Peter was nearly killed? What are the chances?"

"You mean that the guy we figured was an arsonist tried to blow himself up?" Stuart asked. "Can't see it as a likely scenario. Even if he'd killed his ex-wife and suddenly regretted it, that's not the way anyone would end it. Too unreliable, and whatever you say about Peter, he wasn't that."

"Where does that leave us?" I asked.

"Always a good question," Stuart said. "But if we are talking about trying to figure out why Twyla died, we might want to hit pause on that before we walk in and talk to the Mounties. There's more going on here than you and I can understand working from my kitchen table. I'd say this is the time we—okay, maybe you—faced the fact we are amateurs. Let's leave it to the professionals in there," he said, pointing to the RCMP reception area inside the doors. He put a hand on each of my shoulders and pulled me toward him to kiss the top of my head. "You know what? Not everything is our business. Not everything is our problem to solve. Maybe you and me should go back to being ordinary people. You know, like we walk our dogs together. I ask you for dinner, and you say yes."

Close to Stuart, I was surprised by how intensely I felt both contentment and panic. Or maybe it was anxiety that I was, at that moment, close to being content and safe. That wasn't how my life was lived, letting someone else care for me. Everything I did was focused outward on other people and giving them what they needed. The three great kids I'd raised almost entirely on my own. The ladies at Seaview, who needed me to keep a secret. Darlene, who needed her love life put back on track. Chester, who needed the insurance money and a good, secure future. The Co-op I'd set up to keep the store alive and the crafters in the community it supported. The dog I'd rescued. Like so many generations of Gasper's Cove women, I felt most like myself when I delivered, when I was dependable. Some women had been raised to go out for dinner, and some women were the ones who made it.

I knew which kind I was.

So, although I wanted to stand there a little while longer with Stuart, instead, I pulled my keys from my pocket.

"You have a daughter coming home from camp tomorrow. And a small dog who needs to go out," I said. "I'll drop you at home."

After I left Stuart in front of his house, I headed back to my own. I felt distracted and confused. I nearly missed the light on the causeway when it turned red. I came within a quilter's seam allowance from knocking into the bumper of the car in front of me. I tried to concentrate, but somewhere inside, I hurt with the feeling that I'd almost touched something that was not meant for, or belonged, to me. It didn't help the ache in my chest to consider my mistakes. I had thought I had it all worked out. Twyla's death and even the reason for it. However, if poor, now mustache-less Peter hadn't started the fire, and if it turned out that the boat club explosion had been caused by someone else, then that meant only one thing.

There was a killer somewhere out there in Gasper's Cove. And I still had no idea who they were.

CHAPTER TWENTY-EIGHT

I was so preoccupied and unsettled when I pulled into my driveway that it took me a minute to notice the note on my front door. But there it was, a torn yellow sheet of lined paper, fluttering on the branches of the cedar beside the front door, illuminated by the light over the porch.

I climbed the steps watched by Toby at the window, paws on the afghan on the back of the couch, his leash in his mouth. I wondered how long he had been waiting for me like that. I felt guilty. I reached over to grab the note. I recognized the handwriting, stepped under the light, and read it.

Hey, Mom. Sorry I missed you. Back from Halifax. No news yet. Suit was great. Something to do. Be in touch soon. Thanks for the sewing, BTW.

Love, CJ

I tried to think. There was nothing in this message that said "Call me, let me tell you everything, wait 'til you hear this." Those times were gone. I'd been up all night working on that suit, but that had been as close as I could be to being involved. I had no choice but to wait and hear the news when it came and pretend the waiting was fine. Deflated, I opened the door and went into the house.

"Oh, Toby, it's been a long day," I said, hugging the one member of my family who still thought I was essential. "It's late. I'm so sorry. Mommy will let you out, we'll eat."

I put the note on the hall table and walked through to the kitchen. I let Toby out into the yard and opened the fridge. I surveyed the lit shelves and sighed. I was hungry, and I was tired. I pulled a plate out of the cupboard, put Toby's bowl on the counter, and made our dinners. Kibble and a generous piece of leftover chicken for my dog. The rest of the chicken, day-old potato salad, and late-season carrots for me. I searched the mason jars at the back of the top shelf for something to perk up my meal. I was frustrated to be so behind in my canning. By this time of year, I usually had made my blueberry and apricot jams and my crab-apple jelly, if the deer that came into the yard at night had left me any apples on the lower limbs of my tree. By the end of the month, I should have started fermenting my sauerkraut and my dills. But now, all I could find to go with my chicken was half a jar of chowchow, made ten months before. I wondered when my life would get back to normal. I hoped it was soon. Feeling sorry for myself, I closed the fridge door, put Toby's bowl on the floor, and let him in.

When he was settled, I picked up my plate and carried it into the dining room. I pulled back the drapes, and I looked out the front window. The big maple trees out front filled the view. It wouldn't be long before their leaves would be scarlet, then blow away. The end of summer always made me feel wistful. But I reminded myself that when the trees were bare, I'd have the best view of all the seasons, down the hill, to the wharf, and out to the ocean. That was one aspect of the winter to look forward to.

Toby came in from the kitchen and sank to the floor under my feet. While I ate, he slept. When I was finished, I put my cutlery in the center of my plate like my mother had taught me and got up, ready to take my dishes into the kitchen and the sink. Then, outside, I heard a sound. I wasn't sure what it was. The wind? I went back to the window. None of the leaves on the trees were moving, nothing unusual was in the yard. I went to turn away, but suddenly at the edge of my vision, I caught the shadow of something dark heading down the street. I moved closer to the glass to look again. There was no one there. The street and the sidewalk were both empty. Not a person, not an animal. Nothing that was moving.

I knew what it was, and it wasn't a trick of fading light. Right deep in my bones, I knew. I hadn't seen anything, I'd felt it inside, as Rankins sometimes did. We had the sense, brought over with our ancestors from Scotland. When premonitions passed, we knew. Uninvited glimpses of things to come, often unwelcome whispers of impending danger. Experiences we shared only after the fact. None of us wanted to have these feelings. We didn't choose them. But because of who we were, they chose us.

I was shaken. I didn't want to be alone. Not for a whole dark evening. I wanted my family. I had to be with them. I grabbed my keys and my dog, took him out to the car, and then headed out to the north side of the island, to the Bluenose Inn, to Rollie, Catherine, and my son.

The light was fading fast. The headlights turned themselves on. I opened a window for Toby so he could smell the sea. I knew that would help him know where we were going. I felt a little better as I drove. The night was clear and very, very quiet. There was nothing to see but the lights of the houses along the Shore Road, fewer and fewer the farther we went. I relaxed. Toby hung his long nose out the window and collected information from the country smells. It was calm, it was peaceful. My dark feelings began to fade away.

But then, just before we made a turn toward the water, Toby froze. He looked at me in panic, then leapt over my shoulder, all 150 pounds of him, in a desperate scramble to get into the back seat. When he jumped, he knocked me hard up against the steering wheel. The car swerved. For a moment, I was afraid I was going to drive us both into the ditch. Then, I straightened the wheels and crossed over the road, coming to a stop in the parking lot of the look-off above the beach.

I twisted in my seat to look behind me. What had scared Toby like that?

In a minute, I knew.

Out over the water, I saw shooting lights burst high in the sky. Rockets shot up into the black and then fanned out, showering trellises of lime green, shocking pink, and white light down until they were extinguished in the waves.

Toby's acute hearing had heard the missiles go up before they burst, before I could hear and see them myself.

Fireworks.

Fireworks. The only thing my giant golden retriever was afraid of. And here they were, spraying out, one after the other, over and over, in the night sky, shot up from a small island past a point on the end of the beach.

We had arrived on the north side of the island for a light show, a celebration to mark the Labor Day weekend.

I turned off the engine. There was no way I could go anywhere until this was done. Behind and underneath me, I felt poor Toby trying to climb under my seat.

"It's okay, it's okay," I said, trying to soothe him, reaching back to stroke his trembling body. When people considered these displays, why did they not think of what it did to the animals?

We were trapped, with no choice but to wait until the display and the light were over. It lasted a long time. Too long. Every time the sparks fizzled and I thought we were safe, there would be another burst of color in the sky, each spreading wider, illuminating the parking lot where we sat. Finally, the last one went up, higher than any before. It rose, then split into three parts; each of those then divided, exploded, sprayed into stars, then sank into the blackness below.

At last, there was silence. Toby tentatively raised his head and then with relief climbed up onto the back seat. I turned to pat him, then behind us I saw a van parked near the end of the lot and against it, a lone figure leaning against the hood, facing the water.

I knew that van. I got out of my car and walked over. "Hi, Alex," I said. "Enjoy the show?"

I could tell by the shift in his position that Alex had heard me, but he didn't look at me or say hello. Instead, he bent down and put a box, one with levers, exactly like one I had seen on the bench at the boathouse, in a bag at his feet.

I knew what it was. A remote control.

"Those were your fireworks?" I asked. I moved closer to make eye contact with the surveyor. I was interested. "It looked like they were coming from that island, but you were controlling them from here, weren't you?"

Alex laughed, but he kept staring into the night, as if he knew I was there, but he wasn't, not totally. "The last one was the best," he said, "but it was over too soon." He turned to me, as if returning from far away, giving his eyes time to focus and recognize who I was.

"It was really something," I said. "You sure knew what you were doing."

That made him smile. "I love it," he said. "Always have. Anything bright, ever since I was a kid. I used to take wood down on the beach and set it up, bonfires, you know. But this"—his hands swept out toward the ocean where the last flare had landed—"is pretty good too." He studied me, maybe trying to be social, but not quite there. I noticed he didn't ask me why I was out on the look-off alone at night. "I know what you're thinking," he said. "Maybe you're right. That I'm one of those ... what do they call it?"

"A pyromaniac," I suggested. I thought of Rollie, who understood this, not far from where I was now, but not close enough. "That's what they call it. Someone who likes fires."

CHAPTER TWENTY-NINE

Alex stopped and stared at me, hard. He was fully present now.

Why did I say that? Out loud? What was I thinking?

I wanted to take my words back and fast. This is where my smart mouth had landed me. Out in the country, on top of a cliff, alone with a road surveyor who I was now pretty sure was an arsonist on the side. And it was dark. I couldn't even enjoy the view. I tried to control my panic enough to think. If it was me, if I'd been someone who had already lit up an old cottage, ignited a boathouse, and set fire to bike sheds and chicken coops up and down the coast, what would I do with a middle-age busybody? Someone who had discovered his secret and could shut down his firebug operation, or worse. The only sound I could hear was the relentless whoosh of the waves down below. I considered our location. If I was Alex, I'd be thinking about that cliff. It was a long way down.

"Get into the van," he said.

I hated heights, so this was something of a relief. I started to giggle. Like I'd done my whole life whenever I was cornered, but Alex wouldn't know that. He hadn't known me that long.

"What's so funny?" he asked, pulling the long sliding door of the van open. I noticed he did this with one hand. The other one was in his pocket. I didn't like that. I started to laugh louder, right in Alex's face, not able to stop.

This was not the right thing to do. Alex had quite the grip. I found this out when he grabbed me by the shoulder and swung me around, slamming me against the side of the van as he reached inside it to grab a long length of nylon webbing, almost like Toby's leash, but with a ratchet clip for making it tighter in the middle. I knew what it was, we sold them at the store to tradesmen who used them to secure loads in their trucks.

But in this case, the load was me.

Before I knew what he was doing, the webbing was around my neck. I choked and reached up. I staggered off balance from the shock of what was happening. The belt around my neck tightened. I felt Alex's hand on the back of my head. He pushed me into the van. Flat on my stomach on the floor of the van, I could feel him work his hands around my limbs. It took me a minute, then I realized that he was wrapping the long free end of the webbing around my wrists and then my ankles. He worked fast.

In under a minute, I was trussed and trapped.

I couldn't sit up. I couldn't escape. It was clear that if I tried to straighten my arms or my legs, I would only tighten the noose around my neck.

The back door of the van slammed.

I was caught.

Out in the night, I thought I heard Toby bark. He was trapped, too, in the car. I was sure he knew I needed him but couldn't get to me.

I started to cry.

The driver's door opened, then slammed shut. Alex shifted the gears. I could feel the van back up.

"I hope you're not taking this personal," he said, "but you and me are going on a little ride. Out over the water. Thought I was going to do this alone, but guess the universe decided I needed company. I'm sorry, you know. It wasn't about the people, or at least that lady who I didn't know would be there, it was about the building. Seeing it go up."

The van lurched onto the main road and turned, away from the Inn, the Yacht Club, and the road back to Gasper's, toward the most deserted stretch of coast.

"And the boathouse?" I croaked. It hurt to say even so little.

Alex continued, conversationally, as if he wanted to make use of the company the universe had sent him. "The yacht club? That was a good one, all that propane, not like those little jobs I had to settle for along the way. That one I had to do. Wouldn't have done it if that manager hadn't put in the cameras."

It wasn't easy to breathe. I wasn't sure how much of that had to do with the webbing around my neck and how much was because I was overcome with disbelief over what I was hearing. Up to now, everything had seemed so complicated. So much evidence, so many relationships, so much history, but that hadn't added up to anything, not at all. The reason behind all the trouble was here, with me, alone in the night, hurtling toward some unknown destination. A boy who liked to play with matches.

I had to do something. But what? I had nylon webbing wrapped around my windpipe and my carotid artery. Tied up tight around my limbs. I was stuck facedown. My options were limited. I thought of my family and everyone I would leave behind. I waited for my life to flash before my eyes. Then, suddenly, out of the blue, I remembered another car trip. With my kids on this same road. They'd taught me, my children, if you can't be anything else, you can always be annoying.

I knew what to do.

Gently, persistently, taking care not to strangle myself, I braced my body against the wall of the van. When I did this, I found I could move my feet a little. So, I began, best I could, to kick the back of the seat in front of me.

"Hey," Alex said. "Stop that."

"What?" I asked in a small, strangled, five-year-old's voice. "Not doing anything." I had a rhythm now. Bend, kick, bend, kick. It was strangely satisfying.

"I mean it. Stop that," Alex repeated. He stepped on the accelerator. I knew where we were, I could see it in my mind. We were driving too close to the edge. I heard the scrape of metal against the guardrail. If Alex wasn't careful, the van and both of us would go over the edge.

The van picked up speed. That scared me. I felt sick. I thought of Toby shut up back there somewhere, alone. I worked my feet harder.

"That's it." It sounded to me as if Alex was talking through clenched teeth. "You're driving me crazy."

If my neck hadn't been pulled so tight, and my face turning blue, I would have laughed. But I had something else to do first. I started to hum. Over and over, the same atonal tune, in time to the rhythm of my feet on the vinyl back of my already-crazy driver's seat.

"That does it!" Alex yelled. "Stop it, or I'll stop you."

I didn't like the sound of that, but at least the van slowed down and veered off the road. Gravel crunched. We'd pulled over. I heard the transmission slammed into park.

We had stopped. It went dark. The moon was out, but clouds covered it over. It was silent. Alex sat there for a moment and then opened his door.

I felt a rush of cold air.

I could smell the salt, the sea. I could hear the waves. We were closer to the drop down to the rocks than I'd thought.

And then, outside the van, I heard boots slide on stones. Alex opened the side door. It squealed on its hinges. I twisted and tried to wiggle away, pathetically, to try to protect myself from the man I knew was coming for me. I couldn't see him well, but I could feel his shape and his anger.

Then, suddenly, there was his face. Right in front of me, backlit by blinding headlights. Somewhere close by in the night was the sound of tires spinning. Alex heard them, too, and whipped around.

And then we both heard the voice of Officer Wade Corkum of the Royal Canadian Mounted Police.

"Stop right there, Flynn. Hands where we can see them." There was a pause. "Rankin. Check inside."

Rankin?

I held my breath. Alex disappeared. I heard something slam up against the back of the van. Then, the beam of a flashlight and behind it a face I knew well. One with my dark hair and, even though I couldn't see it in this light, one green eye and one blue. He looked so tall to me. When did that happen? When he was away at university? Banking in Toronto? Why hadn't I noticed this before?

"Geez. Mom?" Chester said. "What are you doing back there?"

CHAPTER THIRTY

The second cruiser was not long in coming. When it did, it took Alex away. Wade followed in the car he'd arrived in and dropped Chester and me off at Drummond Consolidated Hospital. They wanted a doctor to look at my neck and make sure I hadn't suffered more than was to be expected from the shock, immediate and delayed.

As soon as we were in the waiting room, I walked up to the triage window. I wanted to know if Peter Tupper had been discharged. The nurse knew me from our sewing classes.

"They let him go this morning," she said. "I heard the girls on the third floor were happy to get rid of him. I guess he has some big ideas for making the healthcare system more efficient." A supervisor walked by, and the nurse stopped talking. When it was all clear, she had a question for me. "Why did you want to see him? He's not your type at all." She looked at the marks on my neck. "And besides, don't you have enough on your plate?"

"It doesn't feel as bad as it looks," I lied. I wanted to stay on topic. "I ran into some nylon webbing, that's all." I knew that dispersing my story to the rest of Gasper's Cove would take care of itself, no need for me to provide more information. "I wanted to talk to Peter because I owe that man an apology. For thinking he was"—I'd almost said "a murderer"—"worse than he is. Plus, I think I have something that belongs to his family."

The nurse raised her eyebrows. Chester shrugged. A look passed between them like an agreement. The nurse got a wheelchair, and my son pushed me away. Going down the hall, Chester pulled out his phone, texted Stuart, and asked him to go to the look-off and pick up my dog.

That made me feel so much better.

The doctor was lovely when we finally got in to see her. She asked questions and examined me with care, but in the end, she allowed me to go home. Stuart came and picked us up. I apologized, because by then it was past midnight, but Stuart said it was fine, that there was no way he could have slept until he heard the doctor's report. Both he and Chester helped me into the car, where I sat in the front seat and tried to adjust to the unfamiliar sound of two people talking about me as if I were the object, not the giver, of care.

Once I was back in my own house, at my kitchen table, watching Chester make us tea, I remembered to ask.

"Your interview? How did that go?"

"Very well, I think," Chester said. "Wade did a great job preparing me. I did okay with the questions. At least, they seemed pleased."

"When do you know?" I asked. Chester stood up and picked up a sponge. He paused before answering, stopping to wipe down the counter, even moving the microwave out to clean under it. When did this kid become such a good housekeeper? I wondered.

"I'm sure it will be fine," I said. "But I have to ask you, how did you and Wade know where to find me?"

"It started with me," Chester said. "I've had my suspicions about Alex for a while. I saw him light a bonfire on the beach earlier this summer. The look on his face when he did it, his excitement, stayed with me. Then, that Kevin guy showed up and started making noises about arson. It made me think."

"In what way?" I asked. "I didn't figure it out. I thought everything was about treasure or a cartoon." I stopped when I saw the look on Chester's face. "I'll explain that part later, or Stuart will. He's got the drawing." I was aware I was losing my train of thought under the strain. "But back to Alex. Who would have thought? He's a firefighter."

"Exactly," Chester said. "He couldn't stay away. Rollie and I were talking. For a lot of arsonists, it isn't the act of starting a fire that gives them the charge. It's the flames, the smoke, the trucks, the noise, the action, the attention. Alex wanted to be there in the middle of the action for all of that. It's why he volunteered with the department. But the problem is that this is Gasper's Cove."

"You lost me," I said.

"There weren't enough fires here to keep him going," Chester explained. "He had to start them himself."

"But as you said, this is a small community. If anyone hung around places over and over that later burst into flame, it would get noticed," I argued.

"Not if you used a remote," Chester held one up. "This is the one Alex used to control the fireworks. Probably he used a similar device to start his other fires. All he had to do was drop off receivers with starters at the sites."

He handed the remote to me. I turned it over. It looked like the one I used for the TV; the only difference was that this remote had a retractable antenna at the top. "You're telling me he planted these spark things all over the place, then turned them on from somewhere else when he wanted the excitement of a fire? Is that it?"

"You got it," Chester said. "The only thing was he had to have an accelerant there too. That's where Peter and the boathouse came in."

"Okay, I don't get the connection," I said.

"Alex kept his kayak in the boathouse. That gave him a reason to be there. It was an easy place to pick up gas. After all, he couldn't keep buying all the bottled gas he needed, that would look suspicious. But who'd pay attention to anyone filling up a gas can on a dock and walking out with a red plastic jug? Nobody."

"But Peter put in a security system, didn't he?" It wasn't a question, it was a statement. "Alex said something about a camera," I added.

"Yup. I guess Peter's a bit of a stickler," Chester said. "He's the kind of guy who would count everything in the building. He put up signs to tell boaters not to take gas cans off the premises. When that didn't work, he put in the camera."

Crafting an Alibi

"Are you saying Alex decided to blow up the boathouse in retaliation?" I asked. "Or was he just trying to kill Peter so he wouldn't tell anyone Alex was taking gas?"

"Possibly," Chester said, "but I don't think Alex ever intended anyone to die." He continued, "That's the thing with compulsions, I guess. According to Rollie, the feeling of an uncontrollable impulse is overwhelming. A person can get so fixated on it that they don't think of the consequences or who they might hurt. I guess what happened with Peter is that he went back to get a list he'd left on his bench. It was the agenda for the end-of-season boat parade, something like that. That put him in the boathouse when it went off." Chester shook his head. "If one of the boaters hadn't left the doors out to the dock open and if Tommy Hirtle hadn't been there, Peter would have been a goner. It was just luck he wasn't the next one."

"Next one of what?"

"Victim of unintended consequences," Chester said. "Like Twyla Waters. That's a tragedy Alex's going to have to live with the rest of his life."

I shuddered. "But how did you put this all together? When Kevin didn't and Wade didn't?"

Chester pulled out his phone and swiped until he found what he wanted. He sat down beside me so we could look at what he had to show me together.

There on the tiny screen, framed in his strong fingers, was a photo of a large map pinned to a bulletin board in an institutional room of some kind, I could tell by the suspended tile ceiling and inset fluorescent lights. I realized the map was of the ocean-side coasts of Gasper's Cove and Drummond. All along the ragged edge of coves, islands, and

195

inlets, someone had placed orange, fluorescent stickers, like little flags. Next to each of these was a small yellow sticky note with a date.

"What am I looking at?" I asked.

"A map and timeline of unexplained fires in the last eighteen months, most small, the biggest the one being at our cottage," Chester paused. "That was around the time Alex joined the fire department. But that's not what got my attention. It was the dates and the routes. A dead giveaway."

I leaned in closer to try to understand what Chester was telling me. "I can't read the notes very well. They're too small."

"It doesn't matter." Chester took his phone from me and put it back into his pocket. "The route is along the same one where we have had a lot of road work. And you know what's even stranger? It starts at the Drummond fire station, and you know where it ends?"

I knew the answer. "Alex's property."

"You got it," Chester's mouth set in a grim, straight line. His face reminded me of my father's. "That explains the route of the fires, but even more interesting are the dates. They are in clusters. All happening the day of, or the day after, a fire Alex would have been at as a volunteer. The way I see it, he'd go on a fire call and then get so jazzed seeing the flames, the trucks, and the excitement that he set fires on his way home, using his starters and his remote. Then there'd be a lull, and it would happen again, and again."

"But back to being there when I needed you," I said. "How did that happen?"

"It was the road work," Chester said. "I was sitting at a stop sign, thinking, waiting for the traffic to be allowed through again, and I realized how many times I'd seen Alex out there surveying on that road. It clicked. I called Wade. He checked it out. The fires began when the road construction did, and Alex was there on the job. A surveyor can set up anywhere. He could start a fire any place where he could drop or throw a starter and, if it needed it, some gasoline."

I listened and picked up my mug. It was one we sold at the Co-op, heavy, with a large handle, the map of Nova Scotia on the side, a tiny heart marking Gasper's Cove, placed where we were, halfway up the eastern shore.

"And the cottage," I said, remembering. "Alex was the one who called it in, first on the scene. He said he saw the smoke, but that wasn't it. He knew there was a fire because he started it."

"Exactly."

"I don't know what to say. The way you explain it, it makes so much sense. But no one else saw this. You did. You saved me. I honestly think that if you and Wade hadn't shown up when you did, Alex and your mother would have gone over that cliff."

My son reached over and held my hand. "It wasn't just me, Mom. It was me and Wade. Good police work. Once we figured out the connection with the road construction, Wade tried to locate Alex. When he couldn't find him, we decided to check along his route home. That's why we found you."

"What happens now?" I asked.

"Alex's in custody. Things will play out there. And me, I'm going to do some follow-up."

"Like what?" I asked.

"Wade checked with the fire department," Chester said. "With all the random fires, they'd been on a campaign to have property owners cut back brush around houses. And guess who the volunteer was who made those visits?"

"Don't tell me, I think I know: Alex." I stopped. "Oh, no, he was at the Inn."

"Don't worry. I've already thought of that. There's a list. We want to make sure Alex didn't leave any remote-control souvenirs behind."

Something in me relaxed. In the morning, I would call Stuart, and we could walk our dogs. My son knew what he was doing.

"What?" Chester asked. "That look on your face? What are you thinking?"

"Nothing much, CJ," I said. "Just that the RCMP will be lucky to have you."

CHAPTER THIRTY-ONE

Peter Tupper held the door to Seaview Manor open. As we crossed the threshold together, I noticed there was something different about him. The pencil-thin mustache was back, although with a few discernible gaps. And only one-and-a-half eyebrows framed his Tupper eyes.

But that wasn't it. The recently exploded manager of the Gasper's Cove Yacht Club had something on his face I had never seen before.

A smile.

"Visiting?" I asked. "Or official business?"

"Tea," Peter said. "With my ladies."

What? His ladies? "Excuse me?"

"Joyce, Bernadette, and Minnie," Peter said, looking past me to wave at the table near the window. "After my folks died, I thought that was it. But did you know that Minnie's mother was my great-aunt's husband's sister on my father's side? We're related."

I understood the smile.

Peter now had family.

"I'm here for the tea party too," I said. "I'm feeling bad. I haven't been in to visit the last few weeks. I wanted to spend some time with my son CJ before he went off to training. He got into the RCMP, you know."

"So I heard," Peter said. "Congratulations. Tommy told me. He's back at the club. I've given him a job on the water. Running the dinghy we keep to take members out to their boats. It was the least I could do after he pulled me out of the drink." He caught himself. "Not that I wouldn't have been able to take care of myself. Caught off guard, got the wind knocked out of me." He touched his missing eyebrow.

"I'm sure you could have." From across the room, Joyce caught my eye. "We better get over there. They're waiting for us."

Minnie was at the head of the table, all dressed up. Her sparkling earrings were a match for her necklace and bracelet, a set I had not seen before. Peter walked over to her and gave his newfound relation a peck on the cheek. He'd brought a round enamel tin with him. He set it on the table. Joyce reached over and snapped it open.

"Oatcakes," she pronounced. "Done just right."

"Of course they are," Minnie said as Peter pulled out a chair next to her and sat down. "The Tuppers were all good bakers."

"How did you figure out the family connection?" I asked. Even for this group of senior genealogists, the relationship sounded complicated.

"It was the ears." Joyce hid her mouth behind her cup to whisper to me. "Who could miss them?"

Bernadette stepped in, more diplomatically. "Last time Peter was in here, we noticed the family resemblance. That got us to thinking. So we went over Min's family tree, and once we found she had a Tupper link, we realized they were related."

"What are the chances?" Peter asked. "I had no idea."

"There are no chances," Joyce said, looking at the tea leaves at the bottom of her china cup. "That's the point."

Peter looked at Joyce. I saw he agreed. "I've been learning a lot of family history," he said. "Very informative."

"And most of it's true," Joyce said for a laugh, then grew serious, stroking Max Factor, who had jumped up onto her lap. "You know, Valerie, that drawing Bernadette gave you? Wrapped around something she kept to herself?" Joyce paused to give Darlene's grandmother a look that needed no interpretation. "It brought everything all together. Maybelline always comes by for a reason. She brings the past. What we need when we need it."

The other two ladies nodded in agreement. Who were they to argue with Maybelline, or with Joyce?

I leaned back in the dining room's upholstered chair while Bernadette filled my cup and passed it over. I took one of the oatcakes from the tin to help me think. Yes, the Tuppers knew how to bake.

"What do you mean?" I asked.

Peter leaned forward. "The Bell cartoon, that's what Joyce means," he explained. "I did some digging in the newspaper archives at the library. Apparently, some old relative of mine ran for office. Casey Baldwin came down and donated the drawing for a fund-raising auction. It was a bit of a novelty. And Casey had a sense of humor. I don't know why it stayed with the family, perhaps someone bid for it. It doesn't matter. What does matter is that they saved it and put it away for safekeeping. If Bernadette hadn't borrowed it when she did, it, an important artifact, a part of Nova Scotia's past, would have been lost."

Minnie's bracelet clinked on her cup. "We told him everything," she explained before I could ask. "And I mean *all*. Since Peter and I are related, it only seemed right."

"There's more," Bernadette said, "Keep going, Peter, tell Valerie what you did." She had been the keeper of the treasure; this was her story too.

Peter offered me the tin. I took another oatcake.

"Once I had the drawing in my hands, I had to decide what to do with it. I felt it was a treasure, but one of historical importance. It was not right for me to keep it for myself. I kept thinking of the Treasure Trove Act of 1954, and what a violation it was for anyone who came across something of value to keep it for themselves without any consideration of the public good. I considered donating it to the province, but I also felt that its guardians deserved some compensation. I found a collector through some contacts in Halifax. He purchased the drawing, but on the agreement that it would be left by his estate, when the time comes, to the Art Gallery of Nova Scotia, and that in the meantime, it would be displayed there in exhibitions as the trustees of the gallery saw fit."

Minnie fidgeted in her seat, ready to continue the story for him. I noticed Peter seemed to enjoy being half of a conversational team. "The money, Valerie," Min coaxed. "Ask about the money."

"All right," I said, "what about the money?"

This was Minnie's moment—it was her family who had provided, who had come through. "Peter gave it to us," she said, "all of us. Split three ways, for our troubles."

"Or maybe the trouble we caused," Joyce muttered, her eyes still on her cup.

"It's not a little bit of cash either," Minnie said. "We're back in business. In time to help out. With back-to-school, Christmas ..."

"And Darlene's wedding," Bernadette added. "Don't forget that. The date is set. Valentine's Day."

"You're right," Joyce said, looking up. "Should be a good one. I wonder, is she registered?"

"Might be," Bernadette responded. "She doesn't have a set of good dishes. I can ask. Maybe. I know she's trying to do it all right this time. Church, white wedding," she smiled at me. "Valerie here's making the dress. Going to be velvet. No one else has the nerves for that job. And the girls at the Co-op are doing the decorations. And I'm doing what a grandmother is supposed to do."

"What's that?" Peter asked, rattling his tin to see if there were any oatcakes left.

"Making sure there is something old, something new, something borrowed"—Bernadette paused and winked at me—"maybe a veil."

"What about something blue?" Minnie asked. "Who's doing that?"

"Sophia," Bernadette said. "Darlene explained it to me. It's traditional in a Greek wedding for the bridesmaids to wear blue. Something about heading off the evil eye. I'm not sure if I got that part right."

"In any case, that sounds like a good idea," Minnie said. "But I wonder, what does that mean?"

Joyce picked up the teapot. "Probably that Kevin Johnson isn't on the guest list," she said.

And she was right.

I didn't know exactly when Kevin had left. No one had seen him go. No one had come out to say goodbye. He went when his work, like his past in our community, was over. After all, when it became apparent that Alex Flynn, not the cottage's insurance policyholders, had set the fires at our place, the boathouse, and many points in between, Johnson Insurance had paid out the policy in full. That meant that CJ and Stuart could start work on plans for a new family retreat, one with solar heating, heat pumps, and a screened-in porch with power outlets in case anyone who came visiting brought her sewing machine.

Stuart was the last person to talk to Kevin before he left town when the so-called investigator had dropped by the office to return drawings of the original cottage he had borrowed. While he was in Stuart's office, Kevin had fished for information about his former spouse, now due at last to have the husband she deserved, someone else. Stuart had refused to gossip, no surprise there, and that left Kevin to try big talk, then small talk, and finally leave, to return to a father who now understood his son worked better under in-house supervision.

Later that month, Stuart and I sat side by side on the bench on the edge of the playground at the end of my street. The dogs were playing. Birdie, young and agile, ran in circles around Toby, who sat and grinned at us, foam hanging from his loose retriever jowls, making sure we fully appreciated he'd made a friend.

"Look at that," I said. "So good for both of them."

Stuart nodded. He had a new leash in his hand and a pocketful of treats. "The best thing I ever did was to get that dog," Stuart said. "Our whole house revolves around him. Erin loves him. He sleeps with her, and when she's at school, he goes back and forth to the window to see when she's coming home. I couldn't stand that he'd be lonely, so I started to take him into the office with me. Bit tough to get him up the stairs past the smells of the restaurant, but he's been good. Only chewed on two of the legs of my desk."

"How does anyone manage without animals?" I asked, picking up the ball Stuart had brought for Birdie and throwing it as far as I could. "You have kids, but they grow up. The house is too quiet. It's important to have someone waiting for you when you come through the door."

Stuart put his arm around me. It was a cool evening. I shivered. "What's the latest from CJ?" he asked.

"He's great, loving training." I looked down to the waves in the cove. "He used to do my taxes, you know, for the Co-op. But a few days ago, he sent me the name of a buddy of his in Drummond who can take over. His CPA days are over."

"Do they know where they'll send him?" Stuart asked.

"When he's done? No idea, probably up north for a bit. But I know eventually he'd like to be posted back here. We'll see. I've got lots to keep me busy. The store, the Crafters. And

Kay is coming from Scotland for Darlene's wedding. Did I tell you that? She's going to be a bridesmaid. That's another dress. Three bridesmaids, the bride, Colleen, and Bernadette. They want silk dupioni and velvet, beaded. That will keep me out of trouble for a while."

Stuart laughed. "You? Out of trouble. We can only hope. Tell me you'll try."

I looked at the empty sky. The last of the fall geese had flown away, gone before the season when the rest of us would go into hibernation for the long quiet months.

"Absolutely," I promised. At the edge of the field, I thought I saw a dark shape. I went still.

"What is it?" Stuart asked.

"Oh, nothing," I said, taking his hand. The dogs stopped playing, noses toward the horizon and the sea. They'd seen, or felt, it too.

Stuart studied the field. "I don't know what you're looking at," he said.

"No, you wouldn't," I answered, moving in closer to him. "You're not a Rankin."

⌣ THE END ⌣

AUTHOR'S NOTE

The drawing done for Casey Baldwin by Alexander Graham Bell was inspired by a real cartoon Bell drew, although the events described in this book are entirely fictional. To me, the whimsical nature of drawing seemed to reflect the humorous and gentle side of life that the community of Gasper's Cove represents.

READER'S GUIDE

Crafting an Alibi

BY BARBARA EMODI

1. When explaining how she and her friends could pull off their heist, Minnie shares "There's power in being underestimated. You can get away with a lot because no one sees you or notices what you are doing." Do you feel that is a true statement? Is it better to be underestimated or capable?

2. In a rare glimmer of insight, Harry notes that while Wade may have missed out on a hockey career, it may also be true that the league missed out on Wade. Do you agree with his assessment? Does Wade remind you of anyone in your life?

3. One of the characters notes that it is "Better to blossom where you're planted." Does this show civic devotion or a lack of ambition? Do you feel these are mutually exclusive?

4. In this story, Valerie wonders why she ends up at the center of everything. She ponders whether it is because she's single, runs a store, because she's naturally nosey, or because of her own insecurity, her need to be needed, that puts her in the vortex. Why do you think so many people to turn to Val? Do you ever feel like this yourself?

5. Do you think Peter was justified in his quest to remove zombie laws from the federal Criminal Code? Can you see any danger in allowing obsolete laws to remain on the books? Which of these pieces of legislation (all real) surprised you the most?

6. Valerie notes that she feels she's an invisible woman. Not young enough to be attractive, therefore too old to matter. Do you feel that this is still sometimes true? Has this aspect of ageism improved in recent years? Do you think the same standard applies to men?

7. Bernadette shares "Your child is your child no matter how old they are. You want to protect them. If they know if you're doing it or not." Do you think many mothers, or mothers-in-law, feel this way? How far is too far when it comes to actions that affect an adult child?

8. At one point Wade explains that his chance to see inside the NFL showed him that, in the end, it wasn't the place for him. His time coaching gifted him with the benefit of hindsight. Is there something you missed out on when you were younger? Would you want the chance to experience it now?

9. Wade advises Valerie to consider Chester's perspective and ambitions. He notes "If he doesn't go for it now it will hang over his head his whole life. ... That's not something you would want to wish on anyone." Have you ever watched someone you care about pursue something that didn't make sense to you? Do you wish you'd said something, or that you hadn't?

10. Valerie is a little frustrated that Chester's generation seems to value the convenience of doing everything on their phones over the quality of the outcome. Have you experienced that same frustration? Do you think the loss of face-to-face conversation is a problem these days or just part of life?

11. Harry has no self-awareness, but Valerie gains more with each adventure. Is it possible to change? Why does she change and he doesn't?

12. At one point in the story George notes that it is impossible to ever really know what goes on in someone else's marriage. Do you agree with his statement? Valerie wonders if George was really talking about Peter and Twyla, or about himself and Darlene. What do you think?

13. Valerie feels that Darlene is often underestimated. She notes "What got missed in all those years of hairdressing and divorcing were the survival skills Darlene collected." Some people call this the difference between book smart and life smart. Do you know someone who fits that description?

14. During the story, Valerie notes that in a small town, actions are often used more frequently than a surface image to imbue trust. "In a small town, if you dig yourself out in a snowstorm to go do the hair of someone's grandmother in hospital, it is remembered." Do you have strong feelings about someone who came through for you, maybe in a small way, that you have never forgotten? What did they do?

15. Secrets were a main theme in this book. Bernadette shares "You keep a secret too long it goes bad, however innocent it was to start with." Do you agree with this? Have you ever kept something secret that was innocent but that ate at you anyway and finally felt like a burden?

16. On the way to the police station, Valerie insists upon driving "I felt that since I'd done all the figuring out, I should be the one to explain it to Wade. Stuart still wanted to come with me and I was glad he did. In a supporting role." Why do you think that Val is adamant about keeping Stuart in a supporting role? Do you understand why she feels this way? If you were her best friend what would you say to her?

17. Stuart advises Val that "Not everything is our business. Not everything is our problem to solve. Maybe you and me should go back to being ordinary people." Do you think that is reasonable to expect of Valerie?

ABOUT THE AUTHOR

Barbara Emodi lives and writes in Halifax, Nova Scotia, Canada, with her husband, a rescue dog, and a cat, who all appear in her writing in various disguises. She has grown children and grandchildren in various locations and, as a result, divides her time between Halifax and the United States so no one misses her too much.

Barbara has published two sewing books—*SEW: The Garment-Making Book of Knowledge*, and *Stress-Free Sewing Solutions*, and she is a course instructor on the innovative and interactive platform Creative Spark Online Learning (by C&T Publishing). In another life, she has been a journalist, a professor, and a radio commentator.

To keep in touch with Barbara, sign up for her newsletter through her website: **babsemodi.com**

And follow her Substack column, How to Be an Older Woman for Beginners.

Visit Barbara online and follow on social media!

Website: babsemodi.com
Blog: sewingontheedge.blogspot.com
Instagram: @bemodi
TikTok: @babsemodi
Fiction website: babsemodi.com/blog-posts
Creative Spark: creativespark.ctpub.com

Gasper's Cove Mysteries Series

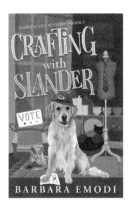

YOUR NEXT FAVORITE

quilting cozy or crafty mystery series is on this page.

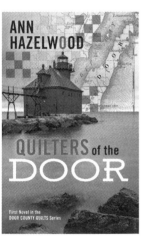

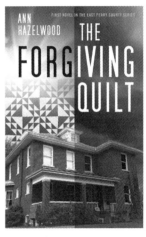

Want more? Visit us online at ctpub.com